I0824515

Books by Edgar Hilsenrath

NIGHT
THE NAZI AND THE BARBER
THE STORY OF THE LAST THOUGHT

and further titles

Fuck America

EDGAR HILSENRATH

Fuck America

Bronsky's Confession

TRANSLATED BY ASTRID KLOCKE

OWL OF MINERVA

Author's website:
www.hilsenrath.de

Publisher's website:
www.owlofminerva.net

Website for this work:

Fuck America
http://doi.org/10.4444/10.4

Owl of Minerva Press
First edition
Berlin 2018

doi: 10.4444/10.4
ISBN 978-3-943334-11-1

Prologue or "Fuck America"

Express Letter
To the American Consul General
Clausewitzstraße 3b
Berlin

November 10, 1938

Dear Mr. Consul General!

Our synagogues have been burning since yesterday. The Nazis demolished my store, emptied out my desk, chased my children out of school, set my apartment on fire, raped my wife, crushed my testicles, confiscated my assets, and froze my bank account. We have to emigrate. We have no other choice. It will only get worse. There is little time. Can you, esteemed Mr. Consul General, provide immigrant visas to the United States for me and my family in the next three days?

Sincerely,
Nathan Bronsky

PS: I have lived in Germany for 40 years, in Halle an der Saale, but I come from Galicia, a province that is now part of Poland.

To the Polish Jew Nathan Bronsky
currently residing in Germany at
Königstraße 10
Halle an der Saale

July 10, 1939

Dear Mr. Bronsky!

Your express letter has been sitting on my desk for eight months. I didn't get around to reading it until today. Enclosed please find some application forms for you to fill out and return to me. Unfortunately, I have to tell you that the chances of a quick immigration to America for you and your family are slim. You see, esteemed Mr. Bronsky, all of a sudden hundreds of thousands of Jews want to come to America. But we can only let in a limited number of them because America is a paradise whose immigration policy has been determined by a cleverly designed quota system since the 1920s. This quota system, esteemed Mr. Bronsky, severely constrains the waves of alien and foreign elements from across the oceans in the interest of a dominant, purely white, Anglo-Saxon, Protestant electorate. The waiting lists for persecuted Jews are therefore long. Very long. Hundreds of thousands of names with quota registration numbers are already marked on the waiting lists. If you fill out the application forms without delay and return them to me, then, at best – given the circumstances – it might be the Bronsky family's turn in about 13 years. I thus estimate, dear Mr. Bronsky, that I will be able to issue immigration visas to you and your family in 1952, provided that you are able, by then, to obtain the necessary affidavits, as well as other pertinent records, vouchers, papers, and documents.

Sincerely,
The American Consul General

To the American Consul General
Clausewitzstraße 3b
Berlin

July 12, 1939

Dear Mr. Consul General!

Time is running out. War is just around the corner. I see terrifying things ahead for us. Please have mercy! I have daily conversations with my stomach ulcer. It tells me strange things: It tells me about gas chambers and firing squads. It tells me about black smoke. The Nazis will murder all the Jews. Us, too. Please have mercy, dear Consul General, and send us the immigration visas as quickly as possible!

Sincerely,
Nathan Bronsky

To the Polish Jew Nathan Bronsky
currently residing in Germany at
Königstraße 10
Halle an der Saale

August 24, 1939

Dear Mr. Bronsky!

Some time ago a Jewish refugee ship tried to land here. It was the well-publicized case of the SS St. Louis. Despite the thousands of telegrams with which our president, Franklin D. Roosevelt, was bombarded, we had no other choice but to chase the refugees, who were not in possession of valid immigrant visas, back out to sea. This goes to show that not even our president, Franklin D. Roosevelt, who – as you may know – is facing considerable political difficulties at home, can afford to simply ignore the anti-Semitic voices of distinct yet numerous groups within the American middle class. Neither can he resist the pressure from the isolationist and anti-Semitic wings in parliament – the so-called "congress" – in order to bring about a change in the immigration quotas to benefit Jewish refugees. So you see, dear Mr. Bronsky, there is no point in burdening me, the American Consul General, with further letters. By the way – between you and me – there isn't a country on this earth that gives two hoots about whether or not they kill you all. The Jewish problem is too much of a bother and no one really wants to deal with it. As far as we are concerned, and by that I mean the country that I represent as Consul General, I can only tell you this: We've had enough of you Jewish bastards in America. You're overcrowding our universities, taking over our leadership positions, and getting more and more impudent. Send back the application forms and wait for your turn in 13 years' time. In case your prophecy about the gas chambers and firing squads turns out to be true, I advise you to write your will now, clearly stating your family's intent to immigrate, so that in 1952, when your immigration visas are ready, the executor of your estate can send your ashes to America as per your request.

Sincerely,
The American Consul General

Diary Entry

New York, March 1953

I dug out my father's desperate letters. As well as the responses from the American Consul General. I read the letters aloud to myself, changing the wording a bit while reading, like I normally do, or to look for the truth written between the lines.

I imagine the Consul General with a bony face and thin, graying, carefully parted hair. When he reads the Jews' letters, his cold blue eyes are set aflame by passion. I wonder if he's jacking off when he tosses the Jews' letters into the trash.

I see a humongous trash can containing the letters of those who have been condemned to death. I see a stream of tears running from the trash can. I hear the voice of the secretary from the room next door: "Mr. Consul General. There's a flood in your office!"

I would like to talk to someone about the Consul General. A suitable location would be the emigrants' cafe at the corner of Broadway and 86th Street. The emigrants there know about it. Everyone there also knows me. Everyone knows: That's Jakob Bronsky, the son of Nathan Bronsky.

How would it be, I ask myself, if the emigrants in the cafeteria didn't know who I was?

This is how I imagine it:

I buy the New York Times on May 22, 1953, to see what's happening in the Korean War. The Times has just been delivered. It's almost two in the morning. I glance over the headlines and notice that they have gotten quieter; I wander down Broadway toward 86th Street. The whores at the street corners know me by sight. "Hey, you old motherfucker. Wanna have a quickie?"

"No, thanks."

"Five bucks. Only five bucks."

"No, thanks."

"How about four bucks? I'll suck you off!"

"No, thanks."

"I'll make it real cheap for you today, boy. Real cheap. 'Cause I got good news. My guy is coming back from Korea. There's talk of peace."

"No, thanks."

The emigrants' cafeteria at the corner of Broadway and 86th Street is open all night. I know the air conditioning is turned off after midnight: The door and windows are then yanked open. But today, strangely, the windows are closed. The main door is open, but just a crack. As I enter, stale air hits me. I see the emigrants. Actually, I'm late, I think. It's already two in the morning. And secretly I'm surprised that the emigrants are still here because they usually go home around midnight.

This is how I imagine it:

No one knows me. Everyone's forgotten that I am Jakob Bronsky, the son of Nathan Bronsky. In the back, at the last table, sits Grünspan, an emigrant who used to be in the textile industry, but here in America he works in sales at Woolworth's, only temporarily, more like a sub, out of work at the moment. Grünspan writes airmail letters and has separated himself from the others. I sit down at his table.

Grünspan pushes the airmail letters aside, as well as the chocolate cake and the watered-down coffee. "My name is Jakob Birnbaum," I say to fool him. "Been in America for a year."

"You're from Germany?"

"Yes. From Germany."

Grünspan nods. He says: "Me, too. From Germany."

This is how I imagine it:

He really has no clue who I am.

I ask: "Have you ever heard of the Bronsky family? From Halle an der Saale?"

"Never heard of them," says Grünspan.

"I happened to know them," I say. "They were from my town."

"Yes," says Grünspan.

"A perfectly normal family," I say. "The old man was a merchant, lived for his business – a furniture store. The wife busied herself in the kitchen. There was also a son: Jakob."

"Also normal?"

"At that time, yes," I say. "Average student. Bad gymnast. Wrote poetry."

"He wasn't normal if he wrote poetry," says Grünspan.

"Perhaps," I say.

"I don't know what became of the Bronskys," I say. "They wanted to go to America after *Kristallnacht* but America's gates were locked."

"Hundreds of thousands wanted to go to America when war was around the corner," says Grünspan, "and America's gates were locked."

"Yes," I say.

"Yes," says Grünspan.

"It's the fault of the Consul General," I say.

"Of the Consul General?"

"Of the Consul General!"

"It's the fault of the American government whom the Consul General represented," says Grünspan. "Or, to put it another way: It's the fault of the American people who elected their government."

"It's the fault of the Consul General," I say.

"Of the Consul General?"

"Of the Consul General!

Guess what became of the Bronskys?"

"I assume they were surprised by the war?"

"You're right about that."

"I assume they were deported by the Nazis."

"That's possible."

"I assume they were gassed in Auschwitz."

"That's possible."

"Or in Treblinka."

"That's possible."

"Or somewhere else."

"That's possible."

"But it's also possible that they were shot by the Nazis," says Grünspan. "Or they starved in a ghetto or in a concentration camp."

"Everything is possible," I say. "It is also possible that they survived the war."

"Possible, yes," says Grünspan. "But unlikely."

"Why would it be unlikely," I say carefully. "After all, others survived the war. You, for example. Or me."

"We are exceptions," says Grünspan.

"Exceptions?"

"Exceptions."

"Let's assume the Bronskys survived the war," I say.

"Okay, let's assume they did," says Grünspan.

"And just how do you think that worked?"

"I don't know," says Grünspan. "I have no imagination."

"I have imagination," I say. "At least, I think I do."

Grünspan laughs. "Okay," he says. "You are a man with an imagination. How did the Bronsky family survive the war?"

"In a trash can," I say.

"In a trash can?"

"In a trash can.

It could also have been three trash cans," I say.

"You're right, three trash cans are better."

"Three trash cans."

"Three trash cans."

I say: "A medium-sized German city. A small, old apartment building. A backyard with three trash cans."

"What kind of people lived in that building?"

"Respectable Germans lived there."

"Opponents of the Nazis?"

"People who were part of the passive resistance," I say. "They knew that the Bronsky family were to be killed and they had resolved to save their lives."

"The lives of three Jews?"

"Three Jews.

Imagine," I say. "How the Jews crouch in the trash cans. They have pulled flour sacks, cardboard boxes, even hat boxes, over their heads. Every morning the sleepy respectable Germans come out of their apartments, empty their trash, chuckle sympathetically but don't say a word. The trash collectors also keep their mouths shut: ex-Communists, also members of the passive resistance."

"A touching story."

"Yes, sir."

"Did the SS stop by?"

"Just once. At night. A single SS man. Dropped off his girl at home. Did it with her in the backyard in front of the trash cans, then pissed on one of the cans in which the old man was hidden, but didn't notice the Jews."

"The girl didn't betray them?"

"No. She didn't betray them.

It only got dicey a few times," I say, "at night when the rats came. Nathan Bronsky wanted to jump out of the trash can."

"Did he do it?"

"No. He didn't do it."

"But the story isn't credible," says Grünspan. "Think of something else."

"Okay," I say. "Let's assume …"

"Let's assume what?"

"That the Bronskys were hiding not in trash cans but in a cellar."

"In a cellar?"

"In a cellar!"

"With the respectable Germans?"

"With the respectable Germans!

They hid out in the cellar for years," I say. "The respectable Germans shared their bread with them, even the janitor, who was a member of the party."

"A Nazi?"

"Not a Nazi."

"Someone who only pretended to be one?"

"Yes, sir.

The old man got depressed," I say. "The cellar broke him. His wife, too."

"And Jakob?"

"I don't know," I say. "Jakob became mute. Didn't say a word for years."

"But he wrote poetry?"

"No," I say. "Jakob didn't write any more poetry.

And then one day the war was over," I say. "The Bronskys stumbled out of the cellar. It was spring."

"Your story's starting to get interesting," says Grünspan. "Keep talking."

"When the Bronskys saw the sun again for the first time in years, the old man wanted to cry but couldn't. His wife also wanted to cry. And Jakob, too. But it didn't work.

'Give me your mirror,' said Nathan Bronsky.

'I don't have one,' said his wife.

'No, you do,' said Nathan Bronsky. 'It must still be in your old purse.'

'I'll look,' said his wife.

'Hurry,' said Nathan Bronsky. 'Find the mirror. It's important.'

Nathan Bronsky looked into the mirror for a long time," I say. "Then he gave the mirror to his wife and to Jakob.

'Our eyes have changed,' said his wife.

'That's right,' said Nathan Bronsky.

'There's no sparkle,' said his wife.

'You're right,' said Nathan Bronsky. 'Our eyes don't sparkle anymore.'

‘I think we lost our souls in the cellar,’ said Nathan Bronsky.

‘I think so, too,’ said his wife.

‘We can look for them,’ said the old Bronsky.

‘In the cellar?’ his wife asked.

‘In the cellar,’ said the old Bronsky.

They returned to the cellar to look for their souls, but they couldn’t find them. They called the janitor. And he came with a flashlight. But he couldn’t find the Bronskys’ souls either.”

“Keep talking,” says Grünspan.

I nod and say: “You see, Mr. Grünspan. That’s what happened.”

“But the story must go on.”

“Of course, it goes on.

I imagine,” I say, “that the Bronskys then went to the Jewish cemetery. There they met a rabbi; he was very old, much older than the old Bronsky, who really wasn’t all that old.

‘Rabbi,’ said Nathan Bronsky. ‘We lost our souls. We looked for them in the cellar, but we couldn’t find them.’

‘Have you searched in your eyes?’

‘Yes, we have.’

‘That’s bad,’ said the rabbi.

‘Yes, it is,’ said Nathan Bronsky.

The rabbi pondered for a while. Then he said: ‘No one can lose his soul.’

‘But we have,’ said Nathan Bronsky.

'It only seems that way to you,' said the rabbi.

'Our eyes have no sparkle,' said Nathan Bronsky.

'That's true,' said the rabbi.

'We lost our souls.'

'No,' said the rabbi. 'You only lost your sparkle.'

'Where's our sparkle?' asked Nathan Bronsky.

'It's up there,' said the rabbi and pointed to heaven.

'Up there?'

'Up there!'

'How could the sparkle just fly away?'

'It didn't fly away,' said the rabbi. 'It just got a lift.'

'With whom?'

'With the six million.'

'The six million?'

'The six million.' "

"What became of the Bronskys when the war was over?" asked Grünspan.

"I don't know," I say. "But I can imagine a few things."

"For example?"

"That they emigrated to America!

The Consul General wrote to Nathan Bronsky in 1939," I say, "telling him that he and his family would have to wait roughly 13 years to get their immigration visas."

"So, they would have been issued in 1952?"

"Exactly."

“Did the Bronskys get their immigration visas?”

“Yes, sir,” I say.

“In 1952?”

“That’s right. In 1952.”

“Keep talking,” says Grünspan.

“Gladly,” I say. “If this doesn’t bore you. The Bronskys are not especially interesting.”

“Tell me,” says Grünspan. “Tell me how the Bronskys went to America.”

“This is what took place,” I say. “One day it happened. One day the Bronskys went to America. 13 years later than planned. With valid immigration visas and no sparkle in their eyes.

They stand at the ship’s rail: Nathan Bronsky, his wife, and his son Jakob.

‘Why are we even going to America?’ said Nathan Bronsky. ‘Now that it’s all over?’

‘I don’t know,’ said his wife.

‘Back when we needed America, the gates were closed. Now we don’t need it anymore.’

‘That’s right,’ said his wife.

‘We might as well go back again.’

‘That’s right,’ said his wife.

When they arrived, thick fog covered the harbor.

‘I would have liked to see the Statue of Liberty,’ said Nathan Bronsky.

‘Me, too,’ said his wife.

‘Why is the Statue of Liberty hiding in the fog?’

‘I don’t know,’ said his wife.

The Bronskys were picked up by a rich relative. He came in a Cadillac.

‘What happened to your eyes?’ asked the rich relative.

‘Nothing,’ said Nathan Bronsky. ‘They lost their sparkle. That’s all.’

The rich relative drove them to Times Square and showed them all the movie theaters lined up side by side; he also showed them 44th Street with its large theaters. Nathan Bronsky saw a black Cadillac that was even nicer than the rich relative’s. The Cadillac was parked in front of one of the large theaters. In it sat a chauffeur in an elegant livery. Nathan Bronsky nudged his wife and pointed to the seedy-looking Negro who stood behind the Cadillac and pissed. He asked the rich relative: ‘Is this America?’

‘Yes,’ said the rich relative. ‘This is America.’

‘I really would have liked to see the Statue of Liberty,’ said Nathan Bronsky. ‘She was hidden in the fog earlier.’

‘Hidden?’

‘Hidden!’

‘You will see her soon,’ said the rich relative.

‘Are we going there?’

‘Yes, we’re going there.’

When Nathan Bronsky saw the Statue of Liberty, he was so shocked he let out a fart: He thought it was the Consul General.

'What's the matter, Nathan?' asked his wife.

'It's the Consul General!' said Nathan Bronsky.

'The Consul General?'

'The Consul General!'

'Are you sure?'

'Absolutely.

I would like to say something to the Consul General,' said Nathan Bronsky. 'But I don't know any English.'

'You know two words,' said his wife.

'That's right,' said Nathan Bronsky. 'I know two words. Two words of English.'

'Then show your knowledge of English to the Consul General,' said his wife.

Nathan Bronsky looked directly at the Consul General. He thought of 1939 and of the Consul General's letter that had dashed all his hopes. And he thought of all the hundreds of thousands of people who had, like him, knocked at the gates of America in desperation, the great land of freedom that didn't want them … back then. And he remembered the feeble excuse involving the quota system. 'Fuck America!' said Nathan Bronsky to the Consul General. He said it very loudly.

'Fuck America?' asked his rich relative.

'Fuck America!' said Nathan Bronsky."

1.

It's busy at Donald's pub on Times Square. Especially in the men's room.

Next to me stands a huge Negro – red scarf, white slouch hat – urinating in a high arc onto the tiled wall above the urinal.

"Tell me, boy. Why are you staring at my black cock?"

"I'm not staring!"

"Yes, you're staring."

"I'm not staring!"

"Yes, you're staring."

"Do you wanna suck it?"

"No."

"Why not?"

"Because."

"Listen, boy. If you don't wanna suck it, then don't stare at it. Got it?"

"I'm not staring."

"Yes, you're staring."

"I'm not staring."

"Listen, boy. For three bucks you can suck it. Now what do you say?"

"Nothing."

"You got three bucks in your pocket?"

"No."

"I bet you haven't been here long."

"That's right."

"Where're you from?"

"Europe."

"Noticed that right away."

"How?"

"Your fly."

"What's wrong with my fly?"

"It doesn't have a zipper. It has buttons."

"Got a problem with buttons?"

"No."

"Well then."

"Where did you buy those pants?"

"In Paris."

"Paris?"

"Paris."

"I used to know someone who had been to Paris. He said it's a great city. Is that true?"

"It's no different from any other city. If you don't have any money, you'll be miserable."

"Like everywhere?"

"Like everywhere."

"But it's still a great city. My friend who went to Paris told me that all French men are pussy lickers. Is that true?"

"Don't know."

"Why not?"

"I just don't."

"I bet you're one yourself!"

"What do you mean?"

"A pussy licker."

"Could be."

"And a smart-ass to boot."

"Possibly."

The big Negro observes attentively as I button up my pants, a bit clumsily but not hastily, as if I was trying to prove that I'm not afraid, trying to appear cool, indifferent but awake, like one of them, someone who comes here after midnight to get a girl or a rent boy, who comes here to piss or to have a beer or both, a Times Square bum, one of the many that sleep during the day and prowl the night for reasons nobody speaks of.

I turn around leisurely, shuffle past the rows of pissing men, watch that I don't slip on the slimy floor and break my neck, I, Jakob Bronsky, who survived the war. That's the last thing I need: to die on this very spot … after everything. Then the newspapers would write: 'War survivor Jakob Bronsky died in the men's room at Donald's! He slipped! He died in his baggy Parisian pants with the old-fashioned buttons … probably bought at the flea market. He died in his cheap American nylon shirt bought at Macy's department store … apparently in the sale. He died in his worn-out black shoes from

Tom McAnn, the inexpensive New York shoe store at the corner of Broadway and 42nd Street. Curiously, no modern Kleenex were found in the pants of the deceased but a dirty, cotton handkerchief, as well as a wallet with 2 dollars and 85 cents, a pencil stub, and a few sheets of writing paper that had been scribbled on. Writing illegible. Apparently German!'

Damn it. Watch out, Jakob Bronsky! – I'm going to make it. A few homosexuals leaning by the door make room and let me pass. Behind me, the bathroom door closes with a snap.

You head directly to the bar, Jakob Bronsky. The largest and cheapest bar on Times Square: Donald's bar. Known. Cherished by all Times Square bums. You could sit near the window in such a way as to keep an eye on it. You will drink a beer, eat barley soup with crackers, smoke a cigarette, and think. While you are thinking, you will stare out the window and observe the masses of people that pass by on well lit 42nd Street, the street of cheap movie theaters, flickering neon lights, traffic jams, snack stands, cafeterias, pimps, prostitutes, homosexuals, silent cops with their big guns. You will sit in such a way, Jakob Bronsky, that you can see the illusory world without being seen.

There are potato pieces and small, pale, slimy mushrooms, like dead fish eyes, floating in the barley soup. The crackers aren't crunchy anymore. The soup is boiling hot. You have to be careful. My fingers grip the beer glass. It's freezing cold.

On the other side of the street, in front of one of the movie theaters, hangs an enormous poster of Humphrey Bogart. Somewhere around here there must also be a film starring the young Elizabeth Taylor. But from my place at the bar, I can only see the Bogart poster, Bogart in the spotlight, grinning in a manly way, cool and superior. "We'll make it, baby. Don't give up! I've got my cock in my hand. Look at my gun. See?"

I sit between two street whores, apparently Puerto Ricans. They look at me disparagingly. One of them is eating a Super Banana Split. Behind her stands a white pimp with a cigar. He winks at me.

"Got a room nearby, buddy?"

"On 75th Street."

"That's too far."

"Yes."

"I've got a room nearby. Three bucks extra. Seven for the girl. Three for the room."

"I'm sorry, Mac. But I'm out of dough."

"Listen, buddy. What do you mean out of dough? How much can you spend?"

"Two bucks."

"You take me for a fool?"

"Nope, not at all."

I finished my soup, ate the crackers, drank the beer. I decide to have a second beer and light a cigarette.

Now I can think without being interrupted. I order a third beer and stare at the dusty bar window.

Listen, Bronsky. Try to remember. During the war. What happened in those days? Damn it. There is a hole in your memory. A dark, abysmal hole. Try to fill it. Pull those events you repressed out of the abyss. At least give it a try. And then write it down.

I take the pencil stub out of my left pocket. Writing paper as well. Take a few notes. Cross a few things out.

At around three in the morning I see the big Negro with the white slouch hat coming out of the men's room. Well, I only really see his reflection in the mirrored wall behind the bar. He sees me and comes over.

"What are you writing, boy?"

"None of your business."

"Wasting your time."

"Could be."

"I made a few bucks in the meantime."

"In the men's room."

"Sure.

How old are you, boy?"

"As old as Methuselah."

"Who's that?"

"Some guy."

"You look like 50, boy. But I think you're younger. I guess around 40."

"I'm younger."

"I don't believe it."

"But I am."

"How young?"

"27."

"Who are you trying to fool?"

"No one."

"Are you Jewish?"

"Yes."

"Do you have a house in Long Island?"

"No."

"How come?"

"Don't know."

"The Jews all have houses in Long Island."

"But I don't have one."

"Why?"

"Because."

"I saw right away that you're Jewish. Earlier, in the men's room."

"How?"

"Your cock is circumcised."

"There are many people with circumcised cocks, even people who aren't Jewish."

"Yeah, that's true.

You got a job?"

"No."

"Why?"

"Because."

"You don't wanna work, right?"

"You're right."

"Why?"

"Because."

"How do you make a living?"

"That's my business."

"You're right."

"Yes."

"But you don't look like a rent boy. Besides you're too old."

"Yes."

"Ever walk the streets?"

"No."

"Why?"

"Because."

"Listen, boy. If you're trying to make a fool of me, I'll sock you one."

"I would advise you not to."

"Can you defend yourself?"

"Yes."

"I don't believe you."

"Believe what you want."

"Don't take offense, boy. Just kiddin'."

"None taken."

"Everyone knows me here at Donald's."

"Okay. Everyone knows you here."

"I was in prison. Had enough of that."

"Okay, buddy."

"Have you been to prison?"

"No. Not yet."

"Why?"

"Because."

"Have you really only been here for one year?"

"Yes. One year."

"Where were you during the war?"

"Over there."

"Over there?"

"Over there."

"Is it true that Hitler gassed the Jews?"

"It is."

"Why didn't he gas you?"

"Was just lucky."

"Did you jump out of the gas chamber?"

"Probably."

"You don't remember?"

"No, not anymore."

2.

At some point, I walked to the subway, put my last token into the turnstile, and went home. When I entered the apartment, I noticed that my landlady was already up. Her bedroom door was open. There was a musty smell in the hallway, noises in the bathroom: splashing, gurgling, a loud fart. I sneaked into my room and locked the door.

I don't know exactly what I dreamt of. It must have been a nightmare because when I woke up around noon, I was soaking wet. I made a beeline for the bathroom. I was taking a piss when it dawned on me that I needed a job.

Bronsky! Listen, Bronsky. It's no joke. You really do need a job. You only have 5 cents left in your pocket. You won't get far with 5 cents, Bronsky, my dear fellow.

Old boy. It's getting serious now. Pay attention. First, you have to shave. Otherwise you won't get a job. But you don't have any razor blades. That's bad luck. But it could be worse. You'll borrow a blade from Mr. Selig next door. He doesn't keep count of his blades. Good. You can also borrow his shaving cream. Just don't take too much. Only a little bit.

And how about breakfast, Jakob Bronsky? Your shelf in the fridge is empty. You could borrow some coffee from Mr. Selig. Pure coffee: Golden Brown, a good brand. Milk, too, of course. He won't notice. Who measures their milk and coffee? Maybe two pieces of toast. That, too. Who keeps count of their toast in America? Nobody! That's right, Bronsky. Nobody. Don't worry, you can do it. Maybe an egg, too? What do you say, Bronsky? Why shouldn't Bronsky also have an egg for breakfast?

You peed. Then you climbed into the bathtub and rinsed off the cold sweat, the cold sweat you woke up with, the cold sweat from the nightmare you can't remember. You shaved, then you had breakfast, naked in the kitchen, with the window open.

So, Jakob Bronsky. Now you should get going. With 5 cents in your pocket. Where to? To the job agency. Where else? You need a job and if you get there in time, you might just get one. Sure. At the agency you'll say: I need a job. Doesn't matter what kind. Just something. The best would be in a restaurant or a bar. A night shift, obviously. I can't wait until tomorrow. Tonight …

Darn it, Bronsky. You forgot that the bus costs 15 cents, as much as the subway! What are you going to do now? You only have 5 cents left in your pocket.

Trying to get a free ride is dangerous. Especially on the subway. The cops are always on the lookout. You can't jump over the turnstile! No, Bronsky. Not on the subway. But on the bus! Of course: the bus!

I'm waiting at the bus stop, corner of Broadway and 72nd Street. Deliberately not standing in line. I wait until the line of people has disappeared inside the bus and jump on after the last one, just as the driver angrily slams the door shut and starts driving. I wait. Not everyone has paid yet. The line of people slowly moves past the driver. I see how he's sweating, the driver. He's driving with one hand, with the other, he hands out change. Accidents are rare. This is New York.

Go on, Bronsky, I tell myself. Stay cool.

Now it's my turn. The driver doesn't look at me but knows I'm there.

"What's the problem, man?"

"Nothing. I'm on the wrong bus."

"Why?"

"Wanted to go to ninety-sixth."

"Then you're really on the wrong bus. I'm headed downtown."

"What do I do now?"

"Dunno."

"Can you let me out?"

"Impossible, man. You have to stay. I'll let you out at the next stop."

"Do I have to pay?"

"No. But you have to get out at the next stop."

"Okay, man."

"You have to take the other bus. On the other side of the street. The uptown bus."

"Okay, man."

This trick is bulletproof. I change buses several times and make it all the way to Times Square. There I get out and walk to Warren

Street, the street that every bum knows.

The building at 80 Warren Street is the meeting point for bums and alcoholics who get their act together every once in a while when their empty bellies start to rumble unbearably or their throats get too dry. The long hallways reek of piss, whisky, sweat, and puke. At 80 Warren Street there are more than 40 private job agencies that arrange the crappiest jobs the big city has to offer, mostly casual jobs or something on some rotten treadmill where they occasionally need a sub. The agencies know their customers and have adjusted their business accordingly. They skim off their profit and make no bones about what it is they offer: jobs for losers, jobs for people who have long stopped dreaming the American dream, or who never dreamt it in the first place; jobs for people without guts, jobs for people who don't belong to a union, have no connections, no references, no profession, and who no longer qualify for the jobs advertised in the New York Times.

I make the usual rounds, walk the long hallways, wind my way through the bums and alcoholics, past the many doors that are plastered with notes. I stop in front of one door. This is the Silberstein agency. I read: SILBERSTEIN'S EMPLOYMENT AGENCY. Bronsky, I say to myself. Silberstein is also an emigrant, someone like you, but someone who's made it in life. A businessman. A small-time crook. But not a bad guy. What matters most is that he knows you. That's important.

Micky Silberstein's office is packed as always. The bums sit dozing on the hard benches. Some of them really are waiting for a job, but most just come out of habit, to beg for a drink, a dime, or a cigarette. The room is smoky: Empty gin and whisky bottles lie on the dirty, spit-on floor covered in greasy sandwich paper and cigarette butts. Silberstein waves as he sees me. He's sitting behind his desk in his shirt sleeves.

"Broke again, Bronsky?"

"'Fraid so, Micky."

"But you've got two dollars, right?"

"No, Micky."

"Sorry, Bronsky. No money, no job."

"You're an asshole, Micky. Acting like I've ever let a debt with you go unpaid. You'll get your two dollars. Tomorrow. Give me a job and you'll get the money tomorrow. Word of honor."

"Alright, Bronsky. But this is the last time."

"Okay, Micky."

"What type of job you want?"

"The night watchman job."

"That's already taken."

"But I saw the note. Outside on the door."

"It's gone, Bronsky."

"How about a waiter position?"

"You a waiter?"

"Yes, Micky."

"You're not a waiter."

"Yes, I am, Micky."

"Have you worked as a waiter before?"

"Yes, Micky."

"Where?"

"In Joe's Clam Bar, Brooklyn."

"Want me to give 'em a call?"

"Go ahead if you don't believe me."

"Joe's Clam Bar. That's a good job. Why didn't you stay?"

"Because I only work casual jobs. I can't stand it too long in one place."

"Do you have black pants?"

"Yes."

"Where?"

"At home."

"And a white shirt?"

"Yes. That, too."

"And a black bow tie?"

"That, too."

"It's a job for one night, Bronsky. As a sub. Good money. Forty dollars guaranteed if you're quick. Tips, of course. A classy job. A waiter's sick. That's the deal."

"Okay, Micky."

"You have to be there at six o'clock. On the dot. Got it?"

"Got it."

"Here's the address. 200 Lexington Avenue. Barney's Steak House."

"Okay, Barney's Steak House."

"You don't need a black jacket. Only pants. You'll get the jacket there. Red jacket with brass buttons."

"Brass buttons?"

"Yes, sir."

"One more thing, Micky, a favor. Lend me two subway tokens. Otherwise I can't get to work. And I have to go home first to get my stuff. Two trips, you understand?"

"I understand, Bronsky."

"Will you lend them to me?"

"No, Bronsky."

"Then I can't get to work."

"Alright, Bronsky. I'll lend you two subway tokens. But this is the last time."

3.

I'd been to Barney's Steak House twice: once in reality, once in a dream. When I started to scream under my blanket, I wasn't all awake yet. Barney's kitchen was up in flames. The steaks were searing and laughing on the grill. The black cook was roaring in terror, with big, wide-open eyes. I see him swinging his cooking spoon and he cracks my head open with his last ounce of strength. "Hey, Bronsky. That was only a gentle warning." I run out of the burning kitchen with my head cracked open. The customers are rioting in the restaurant. "We complained about you to the head waiter and he told us your name. You're Bronsky! The slowest and lousiest waiter in all America! We've already been waiting an hour for our steaks!" – "Please, ladies and gentlemen, I'm here. It just took a while because I have no routine." – "Hey, Bronsky! What's going on? Your head is cracked open. Instead of steaks, there's brain floating on your tray." – "Ladies and gentlemen. You are mistaken. Don't rat me out to the boss. These really are genuine steaks. I have to earn my forty bucks."

The boss calls me into his office at seven o'clock. "You are fired, Bronsky."

"But why, sir? I just started."

"You're still fired."

"But this is a night job. If I'm not mistaken, you don't close this place until three in the morning."

"Yes, you're right."

"But you can't fire me now?"

"Yes, I can."

My boss makes an agitated phone call. "Hello, this is Barney's Steak House!" His wife whispers something in his ear. He slams the phone down.

"You're lucky, Bronsky. The agencies are all closed. I can't find another stand-in now."

"Does that mean I can continue working?"

"Yes, Bronsky. But pay attention!"

His wife puts on a sweet smile. "You're really lucky that all the agencies are closed."

"Yes, ma'am."

"We always serve a Martini with an olive here," says the boss, "not with a cherry. Only sweet drinks are served with cherries."

"Yes, sir."

"Why did you serve the Martini with a cherry?"

"Because I'm near-sighted, sir."

"Okay, Bronsky."

His wife puts on that sweet smile again. "You shouldn't scratch your behind in the presence of the customers either."

"But it was itching, ma'am."

"Then go to the restroom next time."

"Yes, ma'am."

I was absolutely convinced that they'd kick me out at eight for sure, but that's when the dinner peak hour started and neither the boss nor his wife had time for me. They were helping the cook in the kitchen and seemed to have forgotten about me. The only one who constantly had his eye on me was the queer head waiter. But I assume that he didn't report back to the boss about me until just before the end of the shift, and because they needed me in the early morning hours to clear away the dirty dishes, I wasn't fired. I stayed until closing time.

Around four in the morning, long after the place had closed and we were done with cleaning up, the boss called me into his office.

"We should have kicked you out yesterday at seven o'clock in the evening, Bronsky."

"That's right," said his wife.

"Or even at six," said the boss, "right as you came shuffling in."

"That's right," said his wife.

"What nerve!" said the boss. "Who do you think you are? This is not a pizza joint but a first-class steak house. You come shuffling in with a dirty shirt, wrinkled pants, worn-out shoes, and unshaven."

"I did shave, sir, but the blade I borrowed was dull."

"I don't give a shit!" said the boss.

"Your queer head waiter lent me some powder. I powdered my face and the customers didn't notice that I was badly shaven."

"You're right about the powder," said the boss. "But what's that supposed to mean: 'Your queer head waiter'? He isn't queer."

"Yes, sir. He's queer."

"And what about your shirt?"

"The shirt was clean, sir. Only the collar was frayed."

"It was dirty."

"No, sir. It was frayed."

"And your pants?"

"I washed them myself."

"But didn't iron them?"

"No, sir. But I put the pants under my pillow for two nights."

"And your shoes?"

"What about my shoes?"

"Those aren't waiter's shoes. Waiter's shoes are black."

"But my shoes are black, sir."

"They aren't black. You can't tell what color they are."

"I bought the shoes at Tom McAnn's, sir. It's a cheap store. The color comes off after a time. Can't do anything about it."

The boss was furious. "The head waiter told me everything."

"What?"

"We don't just serve steaks in our steak house. You know that quite well. We have an extensive menu. A large selection of dishes. Of course, most people eat steaks because that's what we're famous for, but the customer can order what he chooses."

"Yes, sir."

"You basically refused to serve anything else. You told the customers that they can only get steaks at Barney's."

"That's right, sir."

"Why, Bronsky?"

"Because I can't remember all those dishes, sir. If I only serve steaks, it's easier."

"What an impertinence."

"Perhaps, sir."

"And what about the deal with the salad oil?"

"What salad oil?"

"A customer at table five wanted more oil for his salad, his Barney's Special Salad. But you couldn't find the oil."

"That's right, sir."

"Because the oil wasn't on the table!"

"Correct, sir."

"You didn't know that we have salad oil in the pantry, on the large shelf?"

"I didn't know that, sir."

"You ran into the kitchen during peak time and asked the cook where the oil was, but he didn't have time to answer?"

"Correct, sir."

"You then turned to the dishwasher. You asked him if he knew where the oil was, but the dishwasher is Puerto Rican and doesn't speak any English. He pointed to the soap bottle, which you then grabbed."

"That's right, sir. The liquid soap looked like oil."

"Salad oil?"

"Salad oil!"

"You then gave the customer liquid soap and afterwards the customer threw up."

"That's correct, sir."

"He called the police, filed a claim, and now we're facing a lawsuit."

"I'm terribly sorry about that, sir."

"But that's not all," said the boss. "You also mixed up customers' checks."

"That's possible, sir."

"You wrote down the drinks from table five on the check for table six …"

"Possibly, sir."

"Because you didn't make a note of the table numbers when you took the orders, I guess?"

"I forget to do that on a regular basis, sir."

"What kind of a waiter are you, Bronsky?"

"I don't know, sir."

"Of course, the customers at table six refused to pay for the drinks – because they hadn't ordered them!"

"I can understand that, sir."

"That means we lost money."

"I'm terribly sorry about that, sir."

"And there's something else," said the boss. "Tables eight and nine weren't served at all."

"That's right, sir."

"You told the customers that you didn't have time."

"I really didn't have time, sir."

"The customers then left. A huge loss for us."

"I'm terribly sorry about that, sir."

4.

I got up at three in the afternoon. I went straight to the post office. Sent Micky Silberstein his two dollars in a blue envelope, as well as the two subway tokens. I've got to stay in good with Micky Silberstein. He always gives me a job.

As I left the post office, it started to rain.

I stand shivering in an entranceway.

Bronsky, I say to myself. You mustn't catch a cold. You got a lot planned this week. You have to work on your novel, your novel based on personal experiences, experiences that you have to dredge up – from the abyss – in order to get them down on paper, albeit in a slightly defamiliarized form. You must write, Jakob Bronsky. That is important. You made 47 bucks yesterday, more than Silberstein predicted. 47 bucks! That will keep you afloat for two weeks. Well, you should pay the back rent. But you won't do that. You'll spin your landlady, Mrs. Buchsbaum, some yarn. Think of something. Anything. Tell her you're in line for a good job. She'll wait a bit longer.

I remember how I found the room: "Older Jewish lady seeks quiet tenant with secure employment." I went there right away. Put on a clean shirt and a tie. Didn't forget the jacket or the hat either.

"Are you a Jewish gentleman?"

"Of course. I read your ad in the German-Jewish emigrant newspaper."

"I only advertise in that newspaper. As a precaution. Negroes and Puerto Ricans don't read it."

"You're right about that."

"It is mostly just read by our people. One can be sure. One knows one will find proper tenants."

"I couldn't agree with you more."

"Do you have a job?"

"Of course."

"What kind of job?"

"I'm a salesman."

"Do you make good money?"

"Very."

"I rent out two rooms, an expensive one and a cheap one, but the expensive one is already taken, I'm afraid."

"That's okay."

"I assume you'd rather have the expensive room, a beautiful room with real walnut furniture. But like I said: It's already taken. A certain Mr. Selig, an East European Jew, but that's okay. He speaks German very well."

"I see. That's good to hear. I have nothing against East European Jews."

"He's a decent man, our Mr. Selig. He could almost pass as a German Jew."

"That's really good to hear."

“Like I said: The cheap room is still available. But it’s only a small room. Surely not good enough for you?”

“I could take a look at it.”

“Of course.”

“I like the room. It’s small but cozy.”

“Costs only half as much as Mr. Selig’s room.”

“And that would be?”

“Six dollars.”

“I’ll take the room.”

“Are you sure it isn’t too cheap for you?”

“No, I’ll take the room.”

“You can use the bathroom. The kitchen, too. I’m gone all day because I babysit at my daughter’s.”

“No problem.”

“Mr. Selig is also gone all day. He has a good job.”

“Is that so?”

“Yes. He’s a philologist, you see.”

“And what does he do?”

“He changed profession. Works in a canning factory. In the office, of course.”

“You don’t say.”

“Mr. Selig is a quiet tenant. I told him right when he moved in: no lady visitors!”

“Understood.”

“Are you expecting lady visitors?”

"No. I'm a quiet tenant. I live a steady life."

"That's what I thought."

I hope I didn't catch a cold. The rain has stopped. The sun's rays are breaking through gaps in the clouds. I stroll along Broadway toward 72nd Street. Cars speed by and splash dirty rain water. Every once in a while, I get hit by a splash but it doesn't matter because I'm wearing my stained, black waiter's pants and the sweaty white shirt with the worn-out collar. I'll change later. I'll also take a bath and have breakfast.

In front of the hotel at the corner of Broadway and 73rd Street, a few street whores are hanging out, just out of bed, like me, half-asleep. I also see a pimp stepping out of the entrance. He surveys me as I walk by.

Over there, on the other side of the street, is a large supermarket.

I buy the necessities, most importantly coffee, eggs, butter, bread, milk, and cigarettes. I also buy shaving cream and blades.

I'm surprised to see Mr. Selig home already, then I remember that today is Saturday. Mr. Selig is sitting in the kitchen. Horn-rimmed glasses, bathrobe, slippers. He's older than I am, maybe 40. His family disappeared without a trace in Poland, back then. He thinks Treblinka, but doesn't know for sure.

"Well, Mr. Bronsky. I see you're making breakfast?"

"Yes, my breakfast."

"Did you sleep well?"

"Yes, very well."

"Mrs. Buchsbaum told me that you lost your job as a salesman."

"I lost it right after I moved in."

"That's too bad."

"Yes, it is."

"What are you doing now?"

"I'm looking for something but it's not easy."

"I can imagine."

"Yesterday I worked as a waiter."

"Does one make good money doing that?"

"Excellent. I earned 47 bucks in one night."

"That's a lot of money."

"Yes, I think so, too."

"How does one make so much in one night?"

"Tips, of course. But one also cheats a bit, makes mistakes on the bill, adds in the date, you know what I mean."

"Of course."

"The bosses are crooks. They live off our backs. One always has to be aware of that."

"I couldn't agree with you more."

"I heard that you also write. Is that right, Mr. Bronsky?"

"That's right."

"May one inquire as to what you are writing?"

"Of course. I'm working on a novel."

"A novel?"

"A novel."

"A work of fiction, I presume?"

"No. It's sort of a historical novel, although one has to distort the facts once in a while in order to understand them better."

"Your own story?"

"My own story. Yes."

"Can't you be a bit more precise?"

"I can – I'm writing a story about the war years."

"Do you still remember everything in detail?"

"That's the problem. That's what I'm struggling with.

You see, Mr. Selig, my dear fellow. There is a hole somewhere in my memory. A large, dark hole. I try to fill it in while writing."

"That won't be easy."

"It isn't."

5.

It wasn't until evening that Jakob Bronsky shaved: with his own blades. He took a bath, pissed, and finally had a bowel movement for the first time in two days. He changed clothes, even his socks. He noticed that the socks were clean but one of them, the left one, had a large hole. He said to himself: Doesn't matter, the hole is over the big toe, nobody will see it.

What does Jakob Bronsky do on a Saturday night? He could go to Times Square, to a cheap movie theater, and jack off. He could pick up a street whore. He could go dancing, at the Roseland, for instance. He could go for a walk, up and down Broadway between 72nd and 96th Streets.

After dark, Jakob Bronsky decides that it would make the most sense to go to the emigrants' cafeteria. There he would eat something – something cheap but not bad – he would chat with the emigrants, and later, around midnight, he would slip away – in other words, retreat to the last table to write.

Usually the emigrants sit at the tables on the front row, close to the wide windows that are decorated with plastic cakes. They sit there every night, look out at Broadway all lit up and the west corner of 86th Street, crack jokes about the street whores who roam about, rail about America and the American dream, complain about the large cars, the tasteless food, the terrible coffee, the pointless jobs, curse the money-hungry American women that they can't afford, make plans, plans to return to Europe, talk about the past, but never about the war, talk about the good old times, about the old coffee house "where you got a magazine and whipped cream for your coffee," talk about girls they had back then "for next to nothing … not like here," talk about the large apartments back then, about the servants, their businesses. Back then everything was good: The food was fresh, the flowers were fragrant, the sky was a different blue, and the streets were clean. No Negroes. No Puerto Ricans.

"Mr. Bronsky!" Grünspan waves to me. He's sitting in front of a mountain of airmail letters, alone at a table in the back of the cafeteria. I wave back, first greet the other emigrants at the tables in the front rows, see Mr. Selig, who isn't here every night, exchange a few words with him, make a joke, then move on … to Mr. Grünspan.

"Haven't seen you for a while, Mr. Bronsky."

"Was busy."

"Worked a lot?"

"Not really."

"You hung around Times Square?"

"Exactly."

"As always, I'm here every night, as you can see."

"Airmail letters?"

"Airmail letters."

I say: "Mr. Grünspan. Did you notice something different?"

"Like what?"

"For the first time, I see a woman among the emigrants."

"An acquaintance of Mr. Selig."

"From Warsaw?"

"No. From Vienna."

"Rather old. Don't you think?"

"Probably 60."

"I wouldn't even fuck her blindfolded."

"I believe you, Mr. Bronsky."

"I'd rather jack off."

"You're absolutely right."

Grünspan pushes the airmail letters aside and leans over to me. "I bet, Mr. Bronsky, that the old bag will get laid tonight."

"By whom?"

"By one of the emigrants."

"You think so?"

"I'm absolutely convinced. You see, Mr. Bronsky, for years these emigrants have lived without a woman, except for the street whores, obviously, who they get laid with every now and then. But street whores don't count. They aren't real women. These emigrants want a private relationship, you know, something that is so rare in America, at least for our kind. Private is private. No matter if she's 60 or 20. Doesn't matter. A hole is a hole. No street whore for a change, get it?"

"Yes, I get it."

"They all have a stiff cock. Just look at them. How they stare at the woman! Sniffing like puppies."

I say: "Mr. Grünspan, we really should alert all the 60-year-olds in the New York area. We should tell them to come to the cafeteria at the corner of Broadway and 86th Street."

"You're absolutely right, Mr. Bronsky. Even the 70-year-olds would still have a chance here."

"Them, too?"

"Yes. Them, too."

I get something to eat: vegetable soup, corned beef with cabbage and potatoes, Coca Cola, coffee, and strawberry pie. When I sit down next to Mr. Grünspan, he says: "You seem to be doing well. That's a nice meal."

"I'm not doing badly. I earned 47 bucks yesterday."

"You don't say. 47 bucks."

"Yes, sir."

"So, you'll be picking up a street whore tonight for sure?"

"I don't know yet."

"Why? A young man like yourself?"

"I have to be frugal. I'd like to live off that money for two weeks."

"You'll be lucky to pull that off."

"No, it'll work.

I had actually wanted to watch a film tonight, in one of the cheap theaters on Times Square. Only costs 85 cents. I can still afford that, especially on a Saturday."

"Why didn't you go to the movies then?"
"Because I couldn't decide."
"What did you want to watch?"
"That film with Elizabeth Taylor."
"So you could jack off?"
"Exactly."
"She's got hot tits."
"Yes."
"Marilyn Monroe would be a more suitable candidate."
"She's not my type.

I also thought about going to the 'Roseland.' Dancing. But then I changed my mind."

"The 'Roseland' is such a waste of time."

"That's true."

"I've been there a few times myself to pick up a broad … you know what I mean … but always went home alone."

"I can imagine."

"At first, I thought it was because I was 45. Or because I'm balding. Or because I'm too short. But that wasn't it, Mr. Bronsky. The girls there can sniff you out. They noticed right away that my English was bad, and also noticed that I didn't have any dough, or a car, or a real job. The usual."

"Yes. That's how it is."

"Of course, I also tried it in other places, in other dance bars, you see – there are plenty – even in the Friendship Club over 28, you know, 'The ball for lonely hearts.'"

"With the same result?"

"Always the same. The same shit."

"Yes."

"Only once," says Grünspan, "I almost got a girl to come with me. That was after the dance at 'The ball for lonely hearts.' I invited her back to my place, for a drink, you know. Thought to myself: She's no spring chicken. She needs a good screw. You'll fuck her tonight, get it on with her. Yeah, but then she didn't want to. Just didn't want to come along."

"What did you do?"

"I did nothing. We were standing in front of the dance bar, looking at each other. I asked her: 'Why don't you want to come along?' – 'Because that's not customary,' she said. 'From a gentleman, I expect to be taken out to dinner first, to a show, or both – then we see what happens.' "

"Did you invite that one to dinner?"

"Yes. What choice did I have? I had a hard-on and wanted to go all the way. She noticed that, too, and immediately suggested an establishment, an expensive one, of course. A nightclub with a show and all the bells and whistles. 'Be a good sport,' she said, 'be a gentleman.' So I went with her to the expensive place. Forked out over forty bucks. Forty bucks! Said to myself: 'That's how it is in this country. That's how it's done. First, you have to show the color of your money. Have to prove that you're someone. Then we will see."

"And what happened then?"

"She stuffed her face," said Grünspan. "Watched the show. Drank a lot, too. Then she disappeared. Just like that."

"Forty bucks?"

"Forty bucks."

"Mr. Grünspan," I said. "Have you ever tried it with an emigrant girl?"

"I have."

"With similar results?"

"Yes. They're even worse. Over there in Europe, they would fuck for a cup of coffee. But here it's different. After they've been here for a few weeks, they realize how it works. They want a man, of course. But one with a car, and a good job. They want to go out. In style. No cheap places. Only the most expensive. And going out once is nowhere near enough. You have to take them out a few times before they spread their legs. And that costs a hundred bucks."

"It's more," I said. "You have to spend more than a hundred bucks before a girl like that gets on her back."

"I can't afford that."

I said: "Me neither."

"You know, Mr. Bronsky. I've been in this country for seven years and have not fucked a single girl privately."

"Because you can't afford it?"

"Because I can't afford it."

I said: "Me neither, although I haven't been here for seven years."

"Never fucked a girl privately?"

"Never," I said.

"Always street whores," says Grünspan. "The likes of us can afford those.

At least you know what you're getting," says Grünspan. "No risk. A thing like that won't happen, I mean that you spend forty bucks and get nothing out of it because the girl just disappears. No, Mr. Bronsky, my old boy. There's no risk with street whores. You pay and you have your fun. And it's not really that expensive. A Negro for five dollars, a Puerto Rican for seven, a white one for ten. Fixed prices. No risk.

The Negroes are the best," says Grünspan, "although they're the cheapest. Just recently I had one that was really hot. Pissed all over my bed."

"Yes," I say. "The black girls are hot."

"Some white girls aren't bad either," says Grünspan, "but they usually want to make a quick buck."

"Yes," I say.

"Puerto Ricans fuck the worst," says Grünspan. "It's a real lousy fuck. They're usually fixated on their pimps and hate all other men."

"That's right," I say.

"You gotta be damned careful."

"Yes," I say.

"I would never let a Puerto Rican suck my cock," says Grünspan, "because they are so full of hate. They could easily bite your cock clean off."

"Yes," I say.

I drank several cups of coffee. We talked for a while longer. Then Grünspan left. The other emigrants at the tables on the front rows also gradually began to depart. Some waved at me. By midnight none of them were left. Around one o'clock in the morning, the "night people" arrived. They came from the movie theaters and bars, dance halls and pool halls. The pimps and street whores of the area also slowly started coming in to get something to eat or drink. The cafeteria filled up.

It wasn't until two o'clock in the morning that I began to write. I wrote until dawn started to break outside on Broadway.

When Grünspan returned early in the morning to get coffee, I was just going over what I had written.

"I thought you were long asleep?"

"I was on Times Square," said Grünspan.

"At the movies?"

"At the movies."

"A night showing?"

"A night showing."

"Did you see the film with Humphrey Bogart?"

"No. With Elizabeth Taylor."

Grünspan got himself two pieces of chocolate cake.

"You wrote, Mr. Bronsky?"

"Yes, Mr. Grünspan."

"Mr. Selig told me you were writing a novel."

"That's right, Mr. Grünspan."

"Mr. Selig told me that it has to do with the war."

"Correct, Mr. Grünspan."

"He mentioned something about a hole. A hole in your memory."

"That's right, Mr. Grünspan."

"You want to fill the hole. Is that true?"

"Yes. That's right."

"Are you the hero of the book?"

"Perhaps I am. But I'm writing in the third person, even though the book is autobiographical."

"I see," said Grünspan. "In the third person. So the hero is a man."

"Of course. The hero is a man."

"What kind of a man?"

"A lonely man."

"A jackoff?"

"What do you mean?"

"A lonely man is always a jackoff," said Grünspan.

"But my book has nothing to do with jacking off. It's a serious book."

"That's okay," said Grünspan. "If he's a lonely man, he's a jackoff."

Grünspan got himself a third piece of chocolate cake.

"Does your book have a title yet?"

"Not yet," I said

"None at all?"

"Nope. Not even a working title."

"Call your book: THE JACKOFF!"

"THE JACKOFF?"

"THE JACKOFF."

"A bestselling title," said Grünspan. "If I were you, I wouldn't change it. It's a top-notch title: THE JACKOFF!"

6.

On Sunday in the kitchen, Mr. Selig says to me: "Congratulations, Mr. Bronsky."

I say: "My birthday has long passed."

"I'm not talking about your birthday."

"Oh?"

"I'm talking about the title of your novel."

"How do you know about that?"

"From Mr. Grünspan. Met him in the cafeteria at lunch today."

"He told you about it?"

"Yes. He said: 'The book is now called THE JACKOFF!' "

"That's correct."

"A fabulous title."

"Yes. I think so, too."

"Have you written much yet, Mr. Bronsky?"

"Not much. But I have taken a lot of notes."

As the landlady enters the kitchen, some food catches in my throat.

"You are eating eggs again, Mr. Bronsky?"

"I like to eat eggs."

"It's four o'clock. Is that your breakfast?"

"Yes. My breakfast."

"How about the rent, Mr. Bronsky? You are three weeks behind."

"I'm a bit short on cash at the moment."

"Are you going to pay tomorrow?"

"No. But next week."

"Do you have a job lined up?"

"Of course."

"As a salesman?"

"No. As a waiter."

"Waiters make good money."

"Exactly."

"In which restaurant shall you be working, if I may ask?"

"At Barney's Steak House."

"That is well known."

"Yes, ma'am."

"Have you worked there before?"

"One night. As a sub. But the boss was very happy with my work. He said: 'Bronsky. Next week our head waiter is going to retire. You can have his job.' "

"He must have been really happy with you."

"Yes, ma'am."

"And he hired you directly as head waiter?"

"Yes, ma'am."

In the evening, Mr. Selig accompanies me. We stroll down Broadway toward 86th Street.

"Are you also going to the cafeteria?" I ask Mr. Selig.

"Yes."

"Is your acquaintance going to be there again? The lady from last night?"

"No. Not today. She usually goes to Café Eclair: you know, the emigrant cafe on 72nd Street."

"I know Café Eclair. That's where the emigrants who've made it in America go."

"Correct.

A nice lady," says Mr. Selig. "I've known her for a long time. But like I said, she doesn't like to go to cafeterias, especially not to the emigrants' cafeteria at the corner of Broadway and 86th Street. She claims that going there is a sign of moral destitution. She says: 'There are only bums, do-nothings, or people with bad jobs.' And late at night, as you know, the worst kind of 'night people' go there. No, that's no place for a lady."

"You're absolutely right."

"She also has a good job."

"Really?"

"Yes. She's a fashion designer. Works at a well-known company on 5th Avenue."

"That's quite something."

"Yes. Indeed, it is."

"Mr. Grünspan guessed her to be around 60."

"She's 62."

"And still hot for a cock?"

"Yes."

"Who took her home yesterday?"

"No one."

"How's that? I thought she was hot for it?"

"She was. But you see, Mr. Bronsky, none of the emigrants at the cafeteria has a good, secure job. It would have been beneath her to get mixed up with one of them. She must preserve her prestige."

We stand around at the entrance of the cafeteria for a while, undecided.

"It's still a bit early," says Mr. Selig.

"I'm not hungry yet."

I say: "You could eat something small. Maybe a sandwich with ham and Swiss cheese?"

"I don't eat ham," says Mr. Selig.

"Are you religious?"

"No. Not at all. But I don't eat ham since the Nazis stuffed it into my mouth once."

"When was that?"

"1940. In Warsaw. After Poland had been occupied."

"Did you eat ham before then?"

"Of course. We weren't religious."

I light a cigarette and look into the semi-darkness of the cafeteria, stare through the window, past the colorful plastic cakes. I think: It's not all dark yet on Broadway. Soon they'll turn on the lights inside.

I say: "Grünspan is sitting among the emigrants today."

"Yes," says Mr. Selig.

"Normally he sits separately and writes his airmail letters."

"Airmail letters," says Mr. Selig. "I'd like to know to whom he writes!"

"He doesn't write to anyone," I say. "The letters all come back."

"But he has to be writing to someone," says Mr. Selig.

"He's probably writing to his relatives who were gassed," I say.

"That is possible," says Mr. Selig. I say: "Yes."

"Do you think he's crazy?" says Mr. Selig. I say: "No."

Then we decided to sit with the emigrants after all. I see a man sitting next to Mr. Grünspan: Mr. Weinrot – about fifty, used to be married, six children, a lawyer; now single, wife and kids vanished without a trace in the war. Today he works as a packer in the Garment District. Next to Mr. Weinrot sits Mr. Ginghold, who's not much older than me. Works occasional jobs. He often talks about a bookkeeping class he wants to take, three times a week, evening school, but he can't decide whether to do it. I also see Mr. Rosenfeld from Vienna, a businessman, back then, who has lost hope and can't seem to make his new life here work. Mr. Specht is also here, already 58, jobless like Grünspan, no real motivation to do anything sensible. I assume he had some job at some point and gets unemployment benefits, like Grünspan, who, as everyone knows, sometimes works as a store clerk at Woolworth's. Next to Mr. Specht sits Mr. Liebermann, a door-to-door salesman, then Rosenberg, a German scholar and an educated man like Mr. Selig, the philologist. Rosenberg, the German scholar, is a janitor in one of the large buildings on Central Park West, not far from the Hotel Plaza. I greeted them all, of course, even Goldberg, a half-blind former jeweler who had to give up his trade, Steinberg, a former general manager, Süßkind, a former hotel owner, as well as Victorovitch, a leather specialist who couldn't keep up with the pace of work in the New York factories, and all the others sitting at the long rows of tables in front of the window looking out onto Broadway.

"Now, Mr. Bronsky," says Steinberg, the general manager. "What do you make of this?" He shows me yesterday's newspaper. "Do you believe in the possibility of a real truce in Korea?"

"I won't believe it until it has been declared," I say.

"What does Stalin say about it?" asks Goldberg, the half-blind jeweler.

"Stalin died a few months ago," says Steinberg, the general manager. "On March 5, 1953. Didn't you know that, Mr. Goldberg?"

"No. I didn't."

"Where do you live? On the moon?"

"I don't read newspapers because I have trouble seeing."

"But we talked about it."

"I probably forgot."

"What worries me the most," says Steinberg, the general manager, "is not the war in Korea but the exaggerated fear of Communism here in America."

"Americans are wholly unsuited for Communism," says Rosenberg, the German scholar.

"Exactly," says Steinberg, the general manager. "Like I already said: The fear of Communism is exaggerated. It can only lead to a shift to the right and, ultimately, to a police state. I can feel it in my bones."

"Your bones are a bad barometer," says Rosenberg, the German scholar. "Your outlook is too bleak. And you're overestimating the influence of the right wing of the Republican party."

"But I'm still worried," says Steinberg, the general manager.

"I'm not," says Rosenberg, the German scholar. "We just need a smarter president. That's all. Eisenhower is a soldier but no politician."

"Didn't you vote for Eisenhower last year?"

"I voted for Stevenson," says Rosenberg, the German scholar. "Stevenson is an educated man and an intellectual."

"Did you place a bet?"

"Of course. I bet ten dollars on Stevenson."

"Too bad about the ten dollars. How can you be so naive and bet ten dollars on a loser when the election result was so predictable?"

"An intellectual president has no chance in this country," says Rosenberg, the German scholar.

"That's not true," says Steinberg, the general manager.

"Did you see those grinning Eisenhower posters, shortly before the election? Eisenhower became president because he had a better grin than that intellectual Stevenson. Whoever has a better grin becomes president in this country. That's how it is."

Mr. Selig gets his Swiss cheese sandwich without the customary ham that is usually eaten with Swiss cheese in America. I order a barley soup because I need to save money. I want to make what I have last two weeks! When we sit back down, Steinberg, the general manager, shows me the other headlines in the newspaper. "Well, Mr. Bronsky. What do you have to say about this? Here it is. You see? 'Young girl raped in car! Screams in drive-in theater! Jewish student from Brooklyn robbed of her virginity!' "

I say: "I don't give a shit about the virginity of Jewish students from Brooklyn."

"How do you mean that, Mr. Bronsky?"

"I'm eating my barley soup now."

"Of course, Mr. Bronsky. Don't let me disturb you."

I wipe my mouth, swallow the last grains of barley, and say: "Jewish mothers send their daughters to college to find a husband. That's a given. You know what I mean: a future doctor or lawyer or something. But the girls are clever. They know they won't get married if they fuck around with the boys in college." – I get my old-fashioned handkerchief out of my right pants pocket, the handkerchief made out of real cotton, and blow my nose. Then I say: "So, one of these girls picks out a boy, a future doctor or lawyer or something, goes cruising with him, heads to the drive-in theater, lets him fumble around a bit – they call that 'petting' in this country – a little bit, you see, not too much, not too little, maybe lets him stick his finger in, but not too deep, you see, only a little bit, makes him really horny just to send him packing." I laugh and say: "Everyone knows that boys in college dorms have masturbating competitions. But that isn't everyone's cup of tea. You can't expect every boy to follow the rules of petting. Some go crazy, lose their heads. Just like that."

"What are you trying to say, Mr. Bronsky?"

"I'm saying that the girl got the boy so hot that he forgot the rules of petting. Ripped down her panties and stuck his cock in."

"You mean, Mr. Bronsky, that it was the girl's own fault?"

"That's what I mean."

"Do you approve of the use of force?"

I shake my head. I say: "No."

"What would you have done with the girl, Mr. Bronsky?" asks Liebermann, the salesman.

"I don't know."

"Think about it."

"Students don't want anything to do with me. Why should I think about it?"

"You think the question is redundant?"

"Yes."

"How long has it been since you last had sex, Mr. Bronsky?"

"That's none of your business."

"You jack off?"

"I don't."

"But I'm sure you do. You are, after all, still a young man."

"But I don't do that."

"Then I don't understand why your novel has this new title!"

"THE JACKOFF?"

"THE JACKOFF."

"Word got around fast."

"As you can see ..."

I say: "Mr. Grünspan came up with the title."

"But you like it?"

"I like it and I intend to keep it."

Rosenberg, the German scholar, says: "An enigmatic title! The critics will rack their brains over it."

I say: "I think so, too."

7.

After two weeks, my 47 bucks had shriveled up to next to nothing. But I was happy anyway because I had finished the fourth chapter of my ambitious novel, The Jackoff. I had re-read the four chapters, crossed some things out, changed a few things, and then penciled the words "Fifth Chapter" on a blank sheet of paper.

I remember: When I went to write down the words "Fifth Chapter", I noticed a large brown cockroach on the blank sheet of paper. I flicked it under the table with my finger. Then I quickly wrote "Fifth Chapter", stuffed the paper and pencil into my pants pocket, got up, handed in my meal ticket at the register, paid, and left the cafeteria. Outside a warm drizzle was falling. It was shortly before daybreak and in the east, behind Central Park, the sky was already pale. I strolled down Broadway whistling. The street seemed deserted. I walked slowly without worrying about the drizzle. I somehow felt worn out, exhausted from writing, but strangely happy and relieved. It was as though I could hear my own blood circulating, as if my body had a second voice that only spoke to me whenever my mind was free, free enough to listen. While walking, I noticed that I had a hard-on. I stuck my hand in my pocket, pushing paper and pencil aside. – Bronsky, I said to myself. There's no point in playing with your cock while you're walking. You wrote a lot, night after night in the cafeteria – sparingly, diligently, single-mindedly – at the last table, after the emigrants had left, eating barley soup and drinking coffee. You were awake through the nights, alone with your thoughts, but now you need a woman. You're still a young man. And a man cannot live off bread alone, I mean off barley soup, coffee, and the hole in your memory that you need to fill.

I saw her standing on 80th Street, in front of a closed bar. She was fat and black and at least two heads taller than me. "Hey, little guy, what brings you out here so late?"

"I'm going home."

"I bet you don't have a home?"

"No, I have one."

"Where do you live?"

"On Seventy-fifth."

"In a fleabag?"

"No."

"Wanna take me with you?"

"My landlady doesn't allow that."

"But she's asleep right now."

"I guess you're right about that."

"A good time will cost you seven dollars."

"You're not Puerto Rican. They cost seven."

"But I do something that the Puerto Ricans don't do."

"What?"

"You can fuck me in the ass. Have you ever fucked a woman in the ass?"

"Yes."

"That's something special."

"Really? I didn't know that."

"It's tighter."

"That's true."

"Do you like my ass?"

"No."

"Why?"

"Because I don't."

"It's fat."

"I don't care for fat asses."

"You like them skinny dolls?"

"Yes."

"But I'm not skinny."

"Well, tough luck."

I walked on, but she followed me.

"Can you spend at least five dollars?"

"No."

"Why not?"

"Because I only have four left."

"I'll take four."

"But I can only spend two."

"Why?"

"What else am I going to live off tomorrow?"

"You won't get a girl for two dollars. Not in the whole of America.

You are a damn little motherfucker. Two dollars! What is with you?"

"Nothing."

"And you have a hard-on. Just look at your pants."

"It's not a hard-on."

"Yes. It's hard.

I bet you haven't had a girl in a long time!"

"You're wrong. I have lots of girls."

"You don't look like someone who has a lot of girls."

"I fuck every night."

"Well, you don't exactly look like it."

"I have a steady girlfriend."

"You don't look like someone who can afford a steady girlfriend."

"But I can."

"Someone who only has four dollars in his pocket?"

"I used to have more."

"You little pisser. For three dollars, I'll do you on the street."

"We can go to my place."

"That would cost five."

"Three dollars?"

"On the street."

"Okay."

Every once in a while a car sped along Broadway, but it was all quiet on 80th Street. Only a few drunks snored on the wide steps in front of the brownstones. We looked for an empty spot between two old cars, a green, shabby old Ford and a gray Desoto. I leaned on the green Ford.

"Should I get the thing out?"

"Yes. Do it."

"For three dollars, I can only suck."

"Okay."

"What type of damn pants are these?"

"What do you mean?"

"They don't have a zipper, just buttons."

"That's true."

I was just about to say: Don't hurry so much, this is costing me three dollars – but then I came. Suddenly I saw a thousand cockroaches on a white sheet of paper. I saw my pencil stub between the cockroaches. It wrote FIFTH CHAPTER all by itself. I saw the tables of the cafeteria quiver. The chairs, too. Somewhere Grünspan's airmail letters were blowing in the wind above the quivering old houses on 80th Street. I heard the warm drizzle laugh as the big, fat, black girl spit my semen on the green Ford.

I then went for a stroll through the dark streets of West Manhattan; slowly and lost in my thoughts, I walked in my Parisian pants, with a content, limp cock. I heard the waking sparrows on the rooftops greet the breaking dawn, saw the first light of day, watched the last street whores disappear from the street corners, as if the new day had chased them away. Now I could once again clearly make out the roaring breath of the big city. The first early risers bolted out of their houses and toward the subway shafts. Some jumped into their cars. Parking lots emptied.

I quietly unlocked the front door. There they were, those familiar bathroom noises that indicated that it was six in the morning: splashing, gurgling, a loud fart.

I decided to go straight to bed.

8.

I hadn't slept so deeply and so peacefully in a long time. When I woke up in the afternoon, I remembered the three-dollar street fuck right away, but also the fact that now I only had one dollar left in my pocket.

Bronsky! You really only have one dollar left. One single, lousy dollar. What are you going to do now? You could find a job, of course. But you're not in the mood for that because you have the Fifth Chapter of your novel already all set out in your head and have to start it today so you don't forget it all.

Bronsky! Your compartment in the fridge is empty. You will borrow another egg from Mr. Selig, two pieces of toast, butter, coffee, and milk. But no. That's not possible. Mr. Selig only has two eggs left in the fridge. If you take one, he'll notice.

Bronsky! Watch it! You aren't stupid. Take the toast from Mr. Selig, the butter as well, the coffee, and the milk. But don't take an egg! Take the egg from Mrs. Buchsbaum. She has 16 eggs left in the box. She's sure not to notice if one goes missing.

Bronsky! Since you're having breakfast in the afternoon, you won't need to eat lunch. Makes sense. So you'll only eat dinner. But where?

Bronsky! While you can eat at the cheap restaurants, you can't just leave without paying first because there is always some guy standing guard who's constantly on the lookout and calls the police right away. Cheap restaurants are generally not ideal for bill dodgers. But it's a different story at the fine restaurants. There they respect the guest, one is treated properly – and one can step out to see after one's car, or something. They don't call the police right away.

Jakob Bronsky! You will go to a fine restaurant tonight! You still have one good suit you hardly ever wear because you're trying to keep it in good condition. Get it out of the closet!

Bronsky! The good suit is also from Paris, just like your baggy pants that you wear every day. Only you didn't buy the suit at the flea market; you bought it at the junk dealer near Boulevard St. Michel. An evening suit. It's discolored under the armpits but no one can see it. It's also a bit crumpled.

Bronsky! Mrs. Buchsbaum has an iron. But since you can't iron, you'll have to think of something else.

Bronsky! You will hang the evening suit in the bathroom, next to the tub. Then you will turn on the hot shower, let the water run until the bathroom is full of steam. Hot steam like in a sauna.

Bronsky! Crumpled suits only need hot steam. Then all the wrinkles disappear. Smooth themselves out.

Bronsky! You will borrow some shoe polish from Mr. Selig to polish your old shoes up nice.

Bronsky! Your shirts are dirty. But one, the striped one, is relatively clean. You will wear that one. A tie, too. And don't forget your hat!

After breakfast I took a walk. I thought about the Fifth Chapter, cut out superfluous sentences in my mind, corrected, underlined, pondered my own unique style of punctuation, spoke dialogues out loud, noticed that people were turning around to look, but ignored them, thought about the German language, the language in which I wrote, which was archaic and ought to be simplified, compared it to English, asked myself, "What could Jakob Bronsky change?", thought about sparse prose, extreme brevity, precise expression, skeletal sentences, cleansed of all ballast, sentences that would hit the nail on the head. Today I would start the Fifth Chapter. Today I would write the whole night through. This much was certain. When I got tired from all the walking, I looked for a suitable snack bar where I could rest and also make a phone call, discovered Ricker's coffee shop at the street corner, stepped in, got change for my only dollar, didn't consume anything, said that I wanted to make a phone call, but had to wait until one of the booths was free, then took a seat on the only comfortable stool that was available at the bar and lit a cigarette. Later I stepped into one of the booths.

I called the most expensive French restaurant in New York: Coupole de Montparnasse, corner of 5th Avenue and 56th Street.

"Hello. I would like to reserve a table!"

"For tonight?"

"Yes."

"All our tables are already reserved, monsieur."

"That's too bad."

"I am sorry, monsieur."

"But I have often dined with you and I was always given a table."

"Really?"

"Yes. Indeed, sir."

"What is your name, monsieur?"

"Birnbaum."

"Birnbaum?"

"Birnbaum."

"One moment, monsieur Birnbaum. Maybe there is indeed a table available. You have often dined with us, you say?"

"Correct."

"Will that be a table for two?"

"No. For one person."

"You're lucky. We just so happen to have a table available, not in the mezzanine but in the 'chambre bleue' if you wouldn't mind dining there?"

"That's okay with me."

"But the table is only available after 9 p.m."

"That's fine."

"Would you like me to reserve it?"

"Yes. By all means."
"Birnbaum?"
"Birnbaum."

You can rely on the management of the Coupole de Montparnasse. My table was reserved. Of course. I left my hat at the coat check and entered my false name into the guest book: Jakob Birnbaum.

A friendly man in a spotless tuxedo who had greeted me, Jakob Bronsky alias Jakob Birnbaum, hands me over to the head waiter who is also wearing a tuxedo and looking very serious and respectful. Rows of waiters and busboys are lined up like a guard of honor. We stride between rows of tables, under heavy, expensive chandeliers, move silently on the thick Berber carpet. I see that some guests look up – cool, contemptuous. One lady in a décolleté dress scrutinizes my worn-out shoes that have been polished to a shine, or is that just my imagination? The head waiter purposefully leads me to my table, waits as I hesitate and stop, clears his throat, and then, with a polite gesture, pushes the chair under my rear as I get ready to sit down.

Here I sit. Jakob Bronsky. Dark evening suit, striped shirt, tie, shoes polished to a shine. I don't dare lift an arm so that nobody can see the marks under my armpits. I move my big toe, feel the hole in my sock. Notice the head waiter who has moved away a few feet but doesn't let me out of his sight. He snaps his fingers. A horde of busboys surrounds my table. I look straight ahead, keeping my cool, stick my right hand in my pocket, feel my handkerchief and, behind it, bunched up pant fabric. I nervously play with my cock.

My table is set in no time: two forks on the left, two knives on the right, soup spoon next to the second, an additional knife. No coffee spoon. The water glass is placed exactly at the tip of the outermost knife. Next to the water glass: the wine glass. Next to the wine glass: the champagne flute, a bit askew. One of the busboys hands me an embroidered napkin, a second one serves water with ice cubes, a third one a delicate basket of bread, a fourth one brings a candle and lights it. A waiter in a blue velvet jacket hands me the wine list, a second one the list of hard liquor drinks, a third one the menu, a fourth one pulls out a pencil.

"I'll start with a drink!"

"Of course, monsieur. Might I make a suggestion?"

"No, thank you. I know what I want."

"At your service, monsieur."

"A Martini with extra gin."

"Yes, monsieur."

"No cherry but an olive."

"But, monsieur. Of course. Cherries are not served with a Martini. I assume you are joking."

"Of course. A joke."

"One olive?"

"One olive."

I order a second drink. I pass on the third because I want to write tonight and need a clear head. I notice a fifth waiter who sneaks around my table. Wave to him.

"I would like to eat now. Please call the waiter who served me the

Martinis."

"Would you like another drink?"

"No, I would like to eat now."

"The waiter that served you the Martinis doesn't serve meals. Only drinks, monsieur."

"And who serves the meals?"

"That is my responsibility, monsieur.

May I recommend something, monsieur?"

"You may."

"We have an outstanding Bouillabaisse."

"I know that. I've had it here many times."

"Would you like a Bouillabaisse?"

"No. Not today. I will start with snails."

"Escargots?"

"Escargots!"

"But, of course, monsieur. Soup, too?"

"No soup."

"Of course, monsieur."

"After the escargots, I will take coq au vin."

"Coq au vin?"

"Coq au vin."

Now the head waiter came back to my table. He must have had ears like a lynx because he knew exactly what I had ordered. He nodded to the waiter in the blue velvet jacket and then turned to me. "Coq au vin?"

"Yes, sir. Coq au vin."

"May I recommend a wine that is the perfect accompaniment to coq au vin?"

"Of course."

The head waiter waved over a wine waiter. He pulled out a pencil. "We have an excellent white wine," said the head waiter. "Bordeaux blanc."

"I only drink red wine with meat."

"I see, monsieur, but we always serve white wine with coq au vin."

"But I don't want white wine."

"Then I will recommend one of our champagnes. We have an excellent champagne: Veuve Clicquot!"

"Veuve Clicquot is exactly what I would like."

"Very good, monsieur."

I had no reason to complain. The food was served discreetly, the champagne was uncorked properly. It made a bang but quiet enough so as not to startle any of the guests. The cork didn't hit the ceiling either, or even my head, but instead was skillfully caught by the waiter in his napkin. I didn't drink much champagne because I wanted to keep a clear head. Instead I ate with relish, smoked occasionally, took my time. Later I ordered a cheese platter because that was the done thing … Camembert, Brie, and Gruyère … also a mousse au chocolat, espresso, and a small glass of Armagnac.

The head waiter came to my table frequently and inquired if I liked the food. At one point – I was just drinking my second espresso – I asked him if I could keep my table until 11 p.m. because I was expecting a lady.

"Of course," said the head waiter.

"I'm just worried about my car," I said, "because the parking meter has expired."

"Where is your car parked, monsieur?"

"Close by."

"Then I would quickly check on it, if I were you," said the head waiter, "and put a dime in the meter. We would be very dismayed if you were to be given a ticket, monsieur."

"You're right. I will go outside and take a look."

"Yes, monsieur."

"Please have them bring me another espresso and a glass of Armagnac."

"I will take care of that, monsieur."

"Please do."

I went to the coat check and got my hat. Said: "Be right back." Then I left the restaurant.

Once outside I started to run, but then I noticed that no one was following me.

I walked to Columbus Circle, sat there on a bench, closed my eyes for a while. Then I got up and walked along Broadway toward 86th Street.

It was shortly before midnight and the emigrants at the cafeteria were just getting ready to leave. Their tables seemed dirtier than usual: overflowing ashtrays, smeared cake plates next to plates with meat and vegetable leftovers, sticky compote bowls, empty coffee cups with large, black-brown stains on the rims, bread crumbs everywhere, spots, wet patches. I had no desire to sit down at their table, didn't pay attention to their surprised stares either, looked for Grünspan, finally discovered him at a table near the air conditioning. He was sitting next to Rosenberg, the German scholar, which I found unusual.

"Well, well, Mr. Bronsky. So elegant! I have never seen you in a real suit!"

"The suit is from Paris, Mr. Rosenberg."

"Like the old pants you usually wear?"

"Correct."

"When were you in Paris?"

"Shortly after the war. Before I came to America."

"Is the hat also from Paris?"

"No. I bought this one in Orchard Street."

"You can get cheap things there."

"That's right."

"You must have had a 'date'?"

"No, Mr. Rosenberg."

"I don't believe you. Surely you were at an elegant restaurant with a young lady?"

"I was at an elegant restaurant. But without a lady."

"Really?"

"Yes."

"You seem to be doing well."

"I can't complain."

"You're writing diligently, I hear?"

"I have already written four chapters."

"And when will you start the fifth one?"

"Tonight."

"Will you publish your book in America?"

"I hope to publish it here some day."

"You're writing in German, right?"

"Of course."

"Then you'll have a hard time here. I don't think American publishers will accept German manuscripts, unless you're Thomas Mann or Erich Maria Remarque."

"Yes, it won't be easy."

"You have to publish your book over there first."

"In Germany?"

"Some place where German is spoken. It could also be in Austria or Switzerland."

"That would be the easiest way."

"Then you'd also have a better chance here, once the book has been printed, I mean. Then you can try to sell it here."

"How do you do that?"

"Through an agent. You must have heard about the agent system in America?"

"Yes. I have."

"The agent pre-edits. That's how it is in this country. And if a well-known agent recommends a certain book, then the book has a chance."

"With the publishers?"

"Correct.

Like I said: You have to get your book printed over there first. German literature is not in high demand in this country. And even the best reviews in the German newspapers don't make much of a splash here either. That's how it is. But if a well-known American agent says to his publisher friend: 'Listen. I discovered something, a big hit written in German that is a huge success over there. Could be something for our market. Maybe a potential bestseller,' then he usually bites."

"I will keep that in mind."

"You do that.

Offer it over there first," said Rosenberg, the German scholar. "Where German is spoken. Don't forget that!"

"Yes, Mr. Rosenberg."

"I have good connections over there. And I'd be glad to put in a word for you."

"What kind of connections?"

"I know the cleaning lady in a large publishing house in Hamburg."

"What can the cleaning lady do for me?"

"A lot," said Rosenberg, the German scholar.

I went to the buffet and got a coffee. Bronsky, I said to myself. The coffee only costs a dime. You can still afford that. You don't need cigarettes right now because you still have half a packet in your pocket and that will be enough for tonight. Rosenberg, the German scholar, has good connections. Sharpen your pencil. Start the Fifth Chapter.

9.

Rarely do I make entries in my journal. Most pages are empty, seem mysterious, emanate secrecy: blank, cheap stationery from Woolworth's. Just once, at the end of June, did I decide to make several written remarks. I wrote: Jakob Bronsky finished the Fifth Chapter yesterday, June 23, 1953. THE JACKOFF is coming along. I need a new pencil. I also need a woman. The more I write, the more my cock itches. My need for sex is directly linked to my creative energy and faith in my art. Unfortunately, this doesn't interest the street whores one bit, and the real girls even less. Jakob Bronsky doesn't count. His art is a manifesto that doesn't stir anyone except himself. Jakob Bronsky is a great artist who hasn't been discovered yet.

Made another entry. I wrote: It's not true that love is only a matter of money here. In this country, if you want a girl who doesn't work the streets or clubs, isn't a call girl or the like – one of the "other ones" – as a man you have to exude success and prove it every day. If you, Jakob Bronsky, meet such a girl, she will wonder: Who is Jakob Bronsky? Why does he write in a language that isn't "in" and is only spoken by certain greenhorns? What does he intend to achieve with his scribblings? Probably nothing. What does Bronsky know about the "American way of life"? Does Jakob Bronsky know that only success counts and nothing else? Is he a guy who ruthlessly gets his way but still believes in God Almighty? Does he know that our world is an idyllic one? Does Jakob Bronsky believe in the infallibility of our system? Is he familiar with the ideals of our forefathers who arrived on the first boat, the Mayflower, and what does he think of Coca-Cola culture? Does Jakob Bronsky believe in the American dream? Will he ever own a new car, expensive suits, his own home, or an apartment on the fashionable East side? Will his income ever exceed $ 150 per week so that people can say: He's worth at least $ 150 per week! Will he ever shell out $ 100 just for the hell of it – to show off? Will he invite me to Las Vegas? Does Jakob Bronsky believe in being a member of a Country Club, and what is he doing to become one? Will I have to endure his cock? Is it worth it? And, finally, I want to get married some day because that's what's expected of me. And I want to get divorced one day to collect alimony. Will Jakob Bronsky ever be able to pay alimony, Jakob Bronsky, the old bum who pretends to be 27? No, Jakob Bronsky. Your scribblings don't interest me. Your boner even less. Go run your cock under a cold shower!

Made one last entry. I wrote: Jakob Bronsky lived off the rest of his last dollar for nine days so he could write the Fifth Chapter.

I remember: In the kitchen early in the morning. Rummaging through the fridge. Said to myself: Bronsky. Let the eggs be. It's too obvious. Mr. Selig will notice. Mrs. Buchsbaum as well. Take only toast, coffee, and milk. Maybe some butter and jam. Too bad you didn't wrap up the good cheese from the Coupole de Montparnasse and take it with you. But you couldn't have done that. They would have noticed.

After I had taken my usual creative break in the afternoon – a long walk that even went through Central Park – I decided to get a decent dinner. Where will Mr. Bronsky dine this time? I asked myself. Mr. Bronsky's shoes are still polished, his Parisian suit is in fair condition, his shirt not quite as clean as yesterday, but you can't see that in a restaurant with dimmed lights. His hat is also fine. Yes. That, too.

Bronsky, I said to myself, you could go to one of those fine restaurants again. But you won't do that because – and you have to admit it – you don't feel comfortable there. All those waiters swarming around you. That's not your thing. It'll be best, I said to myself, if you just go to a cheap restaurant this time, although that's dangerous for a bill dodger as you're already aware. You'll just have to risk it. Try one of those cheap Chinese places that you can find on any street corner in New York.

Between seven and eight p.m., I inspected the restrooms of all the Chinese places between 42nd and 59th Street west of 5th Avenue. Finally, I found what I was looking for. A one-stall restroom with a wide, rusty sliding window that led out back. I noticed there was an unlit backyard; an open door in one of the neighboring houses, probably an exit that led out to 6th Avenue. Bronsky, I said to myself, that's the right eatery.

Jakob Bronsky had wonton soup, then beef with rice and soybean sprouts, he drank Chinese tea: jasmine tea.

Then he went to the restroom and didn't return.

The trick with the restroom kept me afloat for a week. I also tried out the Chinese eateries on the East side, a few in Greenwich Village, and a few uptown between 103rd and 110th Street. I didn't want to anger too many Chinese folks, so I tried the restroom trick just once in a steakhouse that belonged to an Irish drunkard who greeted every guest, including me, in person. I nearly got caught there. You see, after dinner, when I went to the restroom to escape, I discovered that the window didn't open. I kept rattling it. Nothing. I started hammering on the window frame but then got scared since I was making so much noise. Bronsky, I said to myself, go try it in the ladies' room. That's your last chance.

I was lucky. The ladies' room was unoccupied. I locked the door, tried the window, thought about how impractical American double-hung windows were, pushed the inner pane up, breathed a sigh of relief, felt my heart pounding, and jumped out.

The backyard was not as dark as I was used to. The windows on the opposite wall were lit. A drunken woman leaned out of one of them. She cursed at me. The Puerto Ricans sat on the fire escapes with their wives and kids. I heard their Spanish gibberish. Someone screamed. A shrill voice. Someone laughed out loud.

I had sprained my ankle slightly in the jump. As I limped through the backyard, I heard the noise of shattering beer bottles that were being thrown down off the fire escapes. I hastily entered the house across the backyard through its rear entrance. A couple of black lovers were leaning against the stairwell. The woman chuckled as she saw me, and the man grabbed my sleeve.

"Hey, buddy, got a smoke?"
"Nope, only a cigarette butt."
"You collect those?"
"Yes."
"I don't smoke that crap."

I had survived for a whole week. I figured I needed two more days to finish the Fifth Chapter. But I'd had enough of the restroom trick.

Said to myself: Bronsky. Try it in a cafeteria. But not in the emigrants' cafeteria because you have to preserve your good reputation there. And anyway that's where you write. You can't piss off the manager there.

Bronsky, I said to myself. Go to the large cafeteria on 34th Street, at the Garment District. You know the place well. There's a meal ticket vending machine at the entrance. The guests each take a ticket, use it to get food and drinks at the buffet, the fella behind the buffet punches the ticket, then they sit down at one of the hundred or more tables, they stuff their faces, drink, then they go back and get more food, again with the ticket, sit down again, sit around for a while longer, and then pay later, on their way out at the register where they hand in the ticket. The thing is, no one can get by the register without showing the ticket.

Usually, the guard hangs out between the ticket machine and the register. His job isn't easy; I almost feel sorry for him. He has to keep his eye on two lines: one that moves along the register toward the exit – to make sure everyone pays – and the other one that pushes through the entrance door – so that nobody takes two tickets.

I waited for the main rush. And just at the right moment, as I was waiting in line with all the people spit out by the clothes factories in the Garment District that were streaming through the entrance of the large cafeteria, the guard was distracted. I saw that he had his back turned to the ticket machine and was yelling at the checkout girl about something she had done wrong. I quickly took two tickets and was pushed on with the crowd.

I had them punch one of the tickets, got some soup, roast with potatoes and vegetables, and later coffee and cake – all with the same ticket. Then, when my belly was full, I tore up the ticket and left. At the register I presented the second, unused ticket.

"Didn't you eat anything, sir?"

"Nothing at all."

"And drinks?"

"No. As you can see, the ticket is unused."

"I apologize."

"Okay."

I did the same thing the following night. After a satisfying meal, I went up to the register and was going to hand the girl the second ticket when the guard suddenly appeared.

"Why do you have an unused ticket?"

"Because I didn't eat anything."

"You took two tickets, didn't you?"

"Can you prove it?"
"No."
"Okay," I said.
"Okay," said the guard.

He ran up to me on the street. "Next time you come in and just sit around without consuming anything, then please don't come during rush hour."
"Okay," I said.
"Okay," said the guard.

I remember: Night after night I sat in the emigrants' cafeteria at the corner of Broadway and 86th Street and wrote like a maniac, with just a few cents in my pocket, a pencil that was too worn down to be sharpened, and a pile of paper. I didn't pay attention to the other customers at the tables around me. Bits of conversations, laughter, the scraping of chairs, the clatter of dishes, and even the distant noises of the street didn't bother me. I didn't notice any of it. I wrote until dawn came through the open front door. Then I got up, a bit dazed and stiff in the knees, but with a happy feeling of accomplishment. I paid a dime for the only cup of coffee I had had, then stepped out onto the street, breathed in deeply and relaxed, looked around for the hookers that had left for the day, strolled down Broadway to 75th Street, went around the corner, and slowly approached the building where I lived.

That morning, when I had completed the final sentences of the Fifth Chapter, I felt a lightness and sense of elation that I had rarely felt before. After leaving the cafeteria, I walked down Broadway whistling, smiled to myself now and then, felt my erection get harder, fiddled sheepishly with the buttons on my pants, walked drowsily in the twilight of the street as though intoxicated.

I don't know what it was but that morning I couldn't calm down my cock. As soon as I got home, I immediately took a cold shower. It made no difference. I thought of Auschwitz. No effect. I went to bed, pulled the covers over my head, didn't roll onto my belly so that I wouldn't excite my cock even more, lay on my back, folded my hands and started praying despite not being religious, and then swore. Nothing helped. "Listen," I said to my cock, "let's have a talk. A sensible chat. We're alone here. I know you want to celebrate because we finished the Fifth Chapter today. We did it. We sweated blood over it. To put it simply: We've both earned a good fuck. But what does it matter? Your master doesn't even have 10 cents in his pocket. Just forget about it. Relax. Go to sleep. I'll also try to get some sleep because this afternoon I will need to get a damn job!"

"But I don't want to relax," said my cock. "The air is hot and humid on the other side of the open window. Can't you think of something for me, Jakob Bronsky? Didn't I help you write the Fifth Chapter? Didn't you magically put it all down? Where did you think your strength came from? Who's behind your imagination? Think about it, Jakob Bronsky!"

Goddamn it! What is it, Jakob Bronsky, that fills you with such longing?

There was this secretary that I would have liked to fuck in the ass. She was a personal secretary with the biggest publishing house in America: Doublecrum & Co.

How did you get to know her? Try to remember how it was, Jakob Bronsky.

This is how it was: I had been in America no more than two weeks and had a job as a delivery boy for a sandwich shop.

"What's your name?" the boss asked when I started there.

I said: "Jakob Bronsky."

"That's too long," said the boss. "Your name is just Jack now."

"Okay," I said. "My name is Jack."

"Listen, Jack," said the boss. "The job is easy. You don't need a college degree for it. You don't need anything to do it. Not even brains. You just have to be able to read. Can you read?"

"Yes," I said. "I can read."

"Okay," said the boss.

"Listen, Jack," said the boss. "The job is really easy. We make sandwiches and coffee non-stop. Got it?"

"Got it," I said.

"Okay," said the boss.

"Okay," I said.

"Listen, Jack," said the boss. "I assume that a greenhorn like you doesn't have much brain mass, no more than a goddamn nigger. But you are probably going to understand what I'm about to explain to you."

"Yes," I said.

"Okay," said the boss.

"Listen, Jack," said the boss. "This job is pretty easy. We get phone calls here all day, mainly from the offices on Madison Avenue. Do you understand?"

"Yes, sir," I said. "I understand."

"The girls in the offices are too lazy to come to our store to buy their sandwiches and coffee. That's why we deliver the sandwiches and coffee to their offices. Do you understand? They call us, place an order, tell us when they want the sandwich and coffee, they give us the exact time when they want the order, that's really important, and we do our best to satisfy them: to deliver right on time."

"With the help of a delivery boy?"

"Correct," said the boss. "You aren't as stupid as you look.

We wrap the sandwich in clean wax paper," said the boss, "we pour the coffee into special paper cups. Then it all goes into a bag with the address and time of delivery on it, understood?"

"Understood."

"But you can read addresses, right?"

"Yes, I can do that."

"Many of the boys can't really read, you know," said the boss. "Especially the damn Puerto Ricans."

"Yes," I said.

"Because these damn boys never really learned English."

"Yes," I said.

"The niggers can all read," said the boss. "But they are stupid and lazy."

"Yes," I said.

"Are you stupid and lazy?"

"No," I said.

"We have ten delivery boys," said the boss. "All niggers and Puerto Ricans. You're the only white boy."

"Yes," I said.

"Our best customer is the personal secretary of Doublecrum & Co., understood?"

"Understood."

"She can't stand niggers or Puerto Ricans."

"Yes," I said.

"Starting today, she is your customer, understood?"

"Understood."

"Because you're a white boy, understood?"

I said: "Understood."

It really was an easy job. After a few days I knew all the servants' entrances and elevators on Madison Avenue between 52nd and 59th Street, the seven blocks that were part of our territory.

Yes. And then there was this personal secretary who didn't like niggers or Puerto Ricans. Maybe she was afraid of them? Maybe she dreamt about their cocks at night? Black and brown cocks are frightening. White women longed for them but couldn't admit it.

And then there was me, Jakob Bronsky, the white boy, whose name had been shortened. Now I was Jack. She wasn't afraid of me. I was harmless. A harmless white boy. Jack. Every day at noon I knocked on her office door.

She was a beautiful woman, neither young nor old, with big tits and big eyes. I never saw her ass because she never got up. She just sat behind her desk, took the bag with the sandwich and coffee, thanked me, gave me a tip – a dime – smiled, looked at me.

She always looked at me when I handed her the bag. Still I noticed that she never saw me. Her smiles went straight through me. During all those weeks she looked at me smiling yet never actually saw me.

And right now I would love to fuck her in the ass.

10.

I imagine that her ass – the one I never actually saw – looks quite normal: just the usual fleshy continuation around the tailbone of a typical personal secretary on Madison Avenue. I imagine that I'm Jack again, the little boy with the sandwich and coffee bag, who is neither a nigger nor a Puerto Rican.

At twelve o'clock sharp, I stand in front of her office door, hold my breath, knock, and enter. There she sits with her big tits and big eyes. Smiling, she looks right through me, takes the bag, says thanks, and pushes over a lousy dime to the other end of the desk for me.

"Why aren't you taking your tip?"

"BECAUSE I WANT TO FUCK YOU IN THE ASS!"

"I beg your pardon?"

"I've never seen your ass because you always hide it behind your desk."

"How dare you use such language with me? I shall complain to your boss."

"I don't give a shit."

"I shall call the police!"

"No, you won't!"

"Why not?"

"Because I have a knife in my pocket."

"You want to kill me?"

"I do! Why do you have such big tits?"

"I don't know."

"And such big eyes?"

"I don't know."

"Why don't you ever see me even though you always look at me?"

"I don't know."

"With your big eyes?"

"I don't know."

"I'm only a sandwich and coffee boy to you. Nothing else. It would never occur to you to study my face. It's not important enough."

"That's right."

"What do you think about when I come to your office every day?"

"About nothing. Oh, no. Wait now: I think of my sandwich and my coffee. I wonder if the coffee is hot and the sandwich fresh."

"That's what you're thinking about when you look at me?"

"That's right."

"And what do you say to me?"

"I say: 'Many thanks. Here's your dime.' "

"You always say the same thing!"

"Yes, always the same."

"And now I finally want to fuck you in the ass!"

"Have mercy on me!"

"No mercy!"

"The publisher could come in."

"I don't give a shit about the publisher."

"He's an important man."

"I'm also an important man!"

"What do you mean?"

"I'm a writer."

"Really?"

"Yes.

And now I finally want to fuck you in the ass!"

"But you haven't seen my ass yet!"

"That's true."

"Because I hide it behind my desk?"

"Very true.

I bet your ass looks quite normal. With a little dimple on the left or the right. I bet you quietly moan when I yank open your ass cheeks. And I bet you scream when I do it: stick my stiff cock in and fill you up. Well, what do you say to that?"

I put my delivery boy hat bearing the company logo on the edge of the desk. I take off my delivery boy jacket with the same logo. I slowly unbutton my shirt, take it off. I'm not bothered by the air conditioning. Then I take off my Parisian pants; my underwear, too. I stand naked in front of the desk. "Well, hurry up!"

Now she gets up, frightened. She slides off her dress. She looks at me, through me. I still haven't seen her ass. Not yet. She would have to turn around first.

There is a knock at the door. I think: That could be the publisher. Doublecrum! Beat it, Jakob Bronsky, before it's too late.

You have to think of something else, Jakob Bronsky. You'll never get to her ass that way. It won't work. You're also not the type of guy to rape a woman. And she would never have believed what you said about having a knife. Think of something else.

Fine, I say to myself. I don't need to threaten her with a knife or to rape her. There are other ways to fuck a girl that just so happens to be the personal secretary at Doublecrum & Company. You could meet her at a party, for example: at a publisher's party?

"May I introduce someone to you? This is Mr. Bronsky. Our new star author. A genius. His book will come out this fall and Mr. Doublecrum is planning a huge launch."

The personal secretary is beaming. Even her big tits are beaming. And her big eyes. She gives me her hand. "Delighted to finally meet you in person, Mr. Bronsky. We've all read your manuscript here. A fantastic book."

"I'm honored."

"Don't be so modest, Mr. Bronsky!"

"But I'm not modest."

"Yes, you are.

We already have a 200,000 dollar film contract for you, Mr. Bronsky."

"I know."

"We've notified all the newspapers."

"The New York Times, too?"

"Of course."

The personal secretary waves to one of the white waiters running around with the drinks. I say: "I was once one of them."

"A waiter?"

"Something similar. I served sandwiches and coffee in a large, brown bag. I was a white delivery boy."

"I don't believe you."

"It's true."

"That must have been a long time ago?"

"Actually, it was fairly recently."

"Forget about it. You're a famous writer now. That's all that matters. To success."

I say: "Yes."

"Let's drink to your success, Mr. Bronsky!"

"Oh well, if it amuses you …

May I accompany you home later?"

"Of course."

"Will you invite me in for a drink?"

"But you just had a drink with me!"

"For a drink in your apartment, I mean!"

"I don't know yet."

"We can get comfortable. And then have some fun. What do you think?"

"You are rather direct, Mr. Bronsky, aren't you?"

"That's my style."

"I have to think about it."

"Okay. Think about it."

My editor takes me aside.

He says: "Mr. Bronsky. I would advise you to leave the personal secretary alone."

"Why?"

"Because she's the lover of your publisher. Mr. Doublecrum!"

"Oh, right."

"That could affect your book. Don't forget that Mr. Doublecrum wants to promote it."

"I think you might be right."

"If Mr. Doublecrum finds out that you're sleeping with his personal secretary, you're history."

"Damn it. You're absolutely right."

Bronsky, I say to myself. You'll never get to her ass, neither as a delivery boy nor as a famous author. It's hopeless.

I imagine myself at this publisher's party: Jakob Bronsky. The star author of the publishing house Doublecrum & Company. Jakob Bronsky surrounded by a bunch of women, both young and not so young … secretaries, editors, as well as ladies of high society and, of course, reviewers, including some from the Herald Tribune and the New York Times. They look at me in awe, wait for me to smile, for a word, for a gracious gesture. Each one of them wants to go to bed with me – me, the man of their dreams, Jakob Bronsky. I could fuck them all, one after another. But I don't want to. Because I, Jakob Bronsky, want one thing and one thing only: the personal secretary's ass.

I leave shortly after midnight. The men nod, the ladies sigh.

There I am, Jakob Bronsky, alone on Madison Avenue shortly after midnight. I've left the party early and I'm annoyed. I've achieved everything I dreamt of for so many years. Only that one dream remains out of reach: the personal secretary's ass.

My Cadillac, which I bought a while ago with my huge advance, is waiting silently by the side of the road. I could get behind the wheel and just drive home to my expensive apartment, not far from here, on Park Avenue. There I could drink an expensive wine – an 1887 vintage – drink generously and at length, then take my clothes off, tired from the wine and slightly unsteady on my feet, hang my expensive two-hundred-dollar suit in the closet, carefully so it doesn't get wrinkled, and then go to bed – but I'm not in the mood for that.

I leave the Cadillac behind and go for a walk. The best way to calm down and forget that unattainable ass. I walk along Madison Avenue, toward downtown. I walk silently and lost in thought.

Suddenly, a car screeches to a halt right next to the lonely walker, Jakob Bronsky. A car door is flung open. I turn around. And who do I see? The personal secretary!

"Mr. Bronsky! I followed you!"

"You shouldn't have done that!"

"I needed to talk to you! I couldn't stand it anymore!"

"Still, you shouldn't have done it. It's too dangerous. What will we do if Mr. Doublecrum notices?"

"Mr. Doublecrum is stewed to the gills!"

"And if someone else notices and tells him?"

"Don't worry. Tomorrow at the publishers I'll tell them I had a headache and that's why I left early."

"And will they believe you?"

"Of course."

I step into the car and join her.

"Where are we going?"

"To my place."

"Don't you want to have coffee somewhere?"

"No. We'll go straight to my place!"

I'm still afraid of Mr. Doublecrum although I'm hungering for her ass. "We could go to Greenwich Village first," I say carefully. "We could go to one of those artists' cafes."

"All you'll find in the artists' cafes in Greenwich Village are failed artists."

"That's true."

"I hate failed artists."

"Really?"

"Yes. They sit all day in some Greenwich Village dive and talk about art. I can't respect those kinds of people. I respect people like you, Mr. Bronsky, who don't talk about art but produce real art."

"Well, you're right about that."

"We're going to my place now!"
"And what about Mr. Doublecrum?"
"Forget Mr. Doublecrum!"

I will fuck the personal secretary in the ass tonight. I'm no longer thinking about Mr. Doublecrum. I've forgotten him. I'm excited. The personal secretary is excited, too. The excitement has made both of us silent. Without saying a word, we drive through the night.

I try not to think about what I've heard about American women from the emigrants. But I still remember:

"Bronsky! Stay away from them! Bronsky! That's not for you. Bronsky! Watch out. This is usually how it goes: First, you have to fork out lots of money because every American woman knows just how much a man has to spend on her. It's all related to their sense of self-worth and their high opinions of themselves and their complexes and their hatred of men, as well as to the status of women in this country and their being raised as precious sexual objects in a conforming society. That's how it is, Bronsky, old boy. And then, Bronsky, my dear fellow, when she's finally willing, you get invited to fuck but you aren't allowed to touch her, at least not right away. And you know why? Because she has to down a few glasses of whisky first to overcome her disgust and her inhibitions and all the fears that have been drilled into her since childhood. That's how it is, Bronsky, old boy. And only then, my dear Bronsky, when the broad is really drunk, then you still can't touch her. Because then she stumbles into the bathroom to take a shower to get sterile. And then she comes out of the bathroom and you still can't touch her. Because then you too have to go to the bathroom to get sterile. That's how it is. And then you come out, naked and clean and sterile, and you still can't touch her. Because, in the meantime, she has sobered up a bit and needs a few more glasses of whisky. That's how it is, Bronsky, old boy. And only then, yes, only then, or a bit later, can you finally fuck her. But it will be a lousy fuck, Bronsky, my dear fellow. A real lousy one."

Don't think about it, Bronsky. It will be different this time for sure. After all, you are Jakob Bronsky, the star author of Doublecrum & Company. And she is the personal secretary.

It's a long, silent drive. She lives in Queens. We leave the Manhattan skyline behind us, the bridges and the East River. Treacherous darkness lies ahead of us on the highway.

Finally, we arrive. She parks the car. She takes my hand. She drags me across the street. She unlocks the front door. Seconds later we zoom up in the elevator. The elevator door flings open. We are standing in front of her apartment.

She unlocks the door. She pushes me into the dark. I fall onto the carpet. She rips my clothes off in the dark.

"Why don't you turn on the lights?"

"No time for that."

"But I would like to see your apartment."

"No time for that."

"And your big eyes. And your big tits."

"No time for that."

"What are you doing?"

"I'm taking my clothes off."

We are lying naked on the carpet.

"Don't you want to drink a few glasses of whisky first?"

"I don't need that. Not when I'm lying on the carpet with Jakob Bronsky."

"You mean with a star author?"

"Exactly."

"And how about a hot shower?"

"No hot shower."

"Should I stick my poet's cock in the front there?"

"You can't, I'm afraid."

"Why?"

"I have my period."

"That doesn't matter to me."

"No, you really can't."

"How do you want to do it?"

"From behind."

"From behind?"

"Exactly."

"I have dreamt about your ass for a long time."

"Really?"

"Yes."

"Wait a moment."

"Why?"

"I have to apply a cream first."

"Where do you keep the cream?"

"In my purse."

"Where's the purse?"

"It's here … on the carpet."

"Is the cream in a box?"

"No, in a tube."

"Can you find the tube in the dark?"

"I've already found it."

"May I help you in any way?"

"No."

"Have you unscrewed the tube?"

"I've already unscrewed it."

"What are you doing now?"

"I'm applying the cream."

"That's taking a long time."

"Not at all. I'm just doing it properly. Okay. Done. Cream applied."

Finally. The hour of truth is here! The minute! The second! Point zero. This is it!

When I come … in my furnished room, with an open window, in my lonely bed, under my covers … that's when I hear the scream of the personal secretary. The East River bursts through the bridges. The Manhattan skyline crumbles. Doublecrum & Company no longer exists. Brown paper bags containing sandwiches and coffee in super cardboard containers float above Madison Avenue. On the street, between car wrecks, lie dead little niggers and Puerto Ricans. Somewhere out there, there is a dead white boy, too. He's holding a woman in his arms who fell onto the street from the crumbling building of the large publishing house; a dead woman with big tits and big, dead eyes: the personal secretary.

11.

Mr. Selig had the flu and had stayed at home. When I came into the kitchen in the early afternoon, pretty hung over and with a throbbing head, he was drinking coffee. My first thought was: Bronsky! You can't have breakfast today. Your box in the fridge is still empty and he will notice if you steal something from the others. That won't work. He has a keen eye.

"I've got flu," said Mr. Selig.

"But it's not that bad. I stayed home, of course."

"I see that."

"How are you doing?"

"I'm doing very well."

"You look pretty hung over."

"Didn't sleep much."

"You look as if you just had a hot night."

"Perhaps."

"Had a girl in your room?"

"Yes."

"Did the landlady notice?"

"She didn't notice anything."

"Are you going to write again today?"

"Not today. I'm broke and need a job."

"Can't do without money?"
"Not for long."
"Do you have something lined up?"
"Yes."

"I heard that there are a lot of jobs now. Is that true?"

I said: "There are always jobs in the summer. Vacation subs. You can always get something."

"Even the bums on Warren Street get work?"

"That's correct."

"You go to Warren Street, right?"

"Yes. I go to Warren Street."

"I went there once, too. In the very beginning. But not anymore."

"Of course. You have a steady job now."

"You can say that again. Most importantly, it's a secure job.

Is it not too late to look for a job now?"

"No. The night jobs aren't handed out until after four o'clock."

"But then you must go soon?"

"I'll get going in a minute."

"You have to shave, too."

"Of course."

I shaved with the last dull blade, took a bath, got dressed, and then immediately took off for Warren Street. Since I didn't have a single cent on me, I took the bus instead of the subway. It wasn't easy but I managed to make it with the usual trick. As it turned out, everything was still right with the world. I was hungry and sensed a slight vertigo, but really, what could happen to me now? No one would deport me to Auschwitz. Silberstein would give me a job. I would work for a night, something, maybe as a waiter again or as a dishwasher or something else. Maybe I would even work two nights or more. I could also get a day job from Silberstein later and hold out for a week or even two, maybe save some money so that I could then write again in peace.

In the days that followed, I worked as a stand-in waiter, dishwasher, kitchen porter, window cleaner, car washer, and packer. Some jobs were at night, some during the day. When I worked at night, I usually got back home tired in the morning and went straight to sleep. But when I worked during the day, I didn't go straight home after work: I hung around on Times Square, sat in Donald's pub, drank beer, ate a hot soup or a Frankfurter, observed my surroundings, talked with the Times Square bums, the street whores, the pimps, took notes, thought about the Sixth and Seventh Chapters, which I would soon write. Every once in a while, I also went to a late-night screening at the movie theater.

Once, at a cheap Times Square theater, I sat next to a white girl. She was clearly one of those who shot up. She sat next to me with wide-open eyes and stared past the bright screen into nothing. She sat there in such a strange way, as if not from this world. Bronsky, I said to myself. She's out of it. She's dreaming with open eyes. Perhaps she doesn't even know she's in a movie theater.

I carefully placed my right hand on her knee. She didn't notice anything. But when I pushed my hand under her dress, she woke up all of a sudden, lifted her head, and pushed my hand away.

Somehow it didn't work out with the jobs. Either I was fired after only a few hours or I made so little that I didn't even go back the next day. One day I decided to talk turkey with Silberstein.

I went to his agency on Warren Street before midday. Of course, Micky Silberstein saw me coming in but pretended he hadn't noticed. The room was crowded in the morning, too. As usual, the bums were sitting on the long benches, dozing. Still, somehow something had changed. I noticed there were no empty whisky or gin bottles on the dirty floor. None of the bums seemed to be drinking today. They sat there, bent over, smoking, waiting. Then I noticed the large sign over Micky Silberstein's desk: NO JOBS FOR DRUNKS!

I quietly took a seat next to the bums, lit a cigarette, and waited.

"Dishwasher wanted!" roared Micky Silberstein. "Super job on Coney Island! Who wants two days of work?"

A few bums got up and shuffled over to Micky's desk.

"Make a line!" roared Micky Silberstein. "Each of you then leans forward and breathes on me. If you're not drunk, you get the job!"

To my left sat a bum in a cowboy hat.

"Well, what do you reckon, buddy?"

"Nothing."

"I bet nobody gets the job."

"Why?"

"Because they're all drunk."

"I didn't see anyone drink?"

"They were already drunk before they got here."

"Perhaps."

"I could get the job but I don't want it."

"Why?"

"Because I can't go all the way to Coney Island. That's too far."

"Yes. You're right."

"Why don't you take the job?"

"Because I don't feel like going all the way to Coney Island either."

I sat between the bums for quite a while. Micky Silberstein had a ton of jobs but they were mostly outside of Manhattan or so badly paid that I preferred to wait. Finally, Micky gave me a sign.

"So, Bronsky. How's it going?"

"I'm fine, Micky. But there's something wrong with your jobs."

"What's wrong with my jobs?"

"They're shitty."

"Okay, Bronsky. I'll give you what I have."

"Recently you've been giving me lousy jobs."

"You're not suitable for the real classy jobs."

"What is that supposed to mean?"

"Remember Barney's Steak House? You royally screwed things up there."

"That was no job for me."

"You're not a real waiter. That's the issue. You screw things up and then I get in trouble because of you."

"Give me a decent waiter job!"

"You mean one where you can earn forty bucks in one night again?"

"That's exactly what I mean, Micky."

"Don't have any, Bronsky."

"I bet you do."

"No, Bronsky. I don't"

For a while, Micky Silberstein rummaged through a stack of loose paper, then fished out a sheet and grinned: "Would you like to work as a doorman?"

"What kind of a job is that?"

"The right job for you, Bronsky."

"What kind?"

"A vacation sub. Three weeks. Night shift. Honest man. Age unimportant. Has to stick with it for three weeks."

"Three weeks is a long time, Micky."

"The job's easy, Bronsky. Think about it."

"I'll take it for three days."

"That's not possible, Bronsky. The job is for three weeks. And you have to stick it out for three weeks."

I took the job. Said to myself: Bronsky! Three weeks is a long time. But you'll just have to stick it out. Maybe it's a good thing. You'll save a ton of money. And then you can write in peace again.

12.

Bronsky! The job is really great. You had no idea how easy doormen have it. No supervisor. No standards to meet. No conveyor belt. Definitely better than those damned waiter jobs. As a night doorman, you don't have to carry any heavy trays or clean away tables; don't need to hurry so that the guests don't run away, don't have to worry about whether or not the bills are correct, don't have any hassle from the bosses and their wives, who always know better about everything and keep a close eye on you, you don't have any fights with the head waiters and the sweaty cooks in the kitchen. Micky Silberstein was right: This is the right job for you.

Bronsky, I said to myself when I was relieved after my first night shift at eight o'clock sharp by the old Irish guy who had been working the day shift for thirty years and whose many years of service had left him a bit soft in the head … Bronsky, I said to myself, this job really is great. The building management gave you a neat, golden-laced livery, as well as a hat with all the trimmings. The building is alright, too. Park Avenue: best part of town. And the tenants, well, they're okay, too.

Bronsky! You really made a wise move here. You start the job at midnight. You have nothing to do. The entrance door is closed. You sit on your lazy ass in the hallway. The chair's comfortable. Everything's fine. Every once in a while someone comes home or a visitor leaves. Then you jump up, greet them politely, and open or close the door. All very simple. Every once in a while you make the rounds, check the air conditioning, the elevator, the electrical fuses, have a listen to see if there is any movement in the basement, look through one of the rear hallway windows out onto the fire escape – purely a precautionary measure. Nothing more.

Bronsky, I said to myself. Who might all these pretty girls be who come into the hallway in their night gowns late at night and slip you tips? Are those the call girls the old Irish guy talked about? The ones who live here in this posh building? Isn't prostitution strictly forbidden in America?

Bronsky, I said to myself. There are a lot of strange visitors after midnight. They are well dressed, wear light-colored summer hats, fashionable suits, and colorful ties. Are they customers of the call girls or their pimps? Hard to tell. They also give you money to keep your mouth shut, and you're not supposed to let them in without carefully checking where they're going and whom they've come to see.

Bronsky, I said to myself: You will not notify the building management. It's none of your business after all. And the old Irish guy keeps his mouth shut, too. And he's been here for thirty years and is a bit soft in the head.

One night three men rang the bell. They were dressed well, and I thought to myself: Surely you can let them in. No doubt they've come to see the call girls. So I opened the door.

Too late. The three were armed. The first one, a white guy, held a gun up to my mouth; the second one, a Puerto Rican, pulled a long knife; the third one, a Negro, had a hammer.

"So, you little motherfucker," said the Negro. "If you don't do what we tell you, you'll be stone dead."

"I'll do anything you say."

"Okay," said the Negro.

"Listen, you son of a bitch," said the white guy. "We'll take the elevator and go on a little ride."

"Where to?" I asked.

"You'll soon find out, you little motherfucker," said the Negro.

First, they wanted to drag me onto the roof, but then the Negro said that the basement would be better. So then we rode the elevator to the basement.

I was sure they would kill me. Bronsky, I said to myself. Your final hour has come. These guys will finish what the Nazis couldn't.

They pushed me into the basement. They took my wallet, searched through all the pockets of my livery, took my shoes off, and searched for hidden dollars in my socks, too.

"22 dollars," said the Negro, who had been searching through my wallet.

"Don't you have anymore?" asked the white guy.

"That's all," I said.

They dragged me into the room with the washing machines that the tenants used for the bargain price of 25 cents. This is the end, I thought. They will cut you into pieces and stuff you into one of the washing machines. Tomorrow morning, or maybe tomorrow afternoon, people will find pieces of you. How could you be so stupid to work as a night doorman in New York? This is a dangerous job.

I had to lie down on the floor and cross my arms behind my back. In a strange way I was less afraid than back during the war; on the freight trains, on the way to where the final solution would be played out. For a few seconds I thought of my mother and what she would say if she knew. I also thought about the Sixth Chapter, which hadn't been written yet.

They tied up my legs and arms. They gagged me and rolled me in between the washers. Then they disappeared in the elevator.

The next morning the old Irish guy, who was already a bit soft in the head from doing the job for so long, found me. He freed me from my fetters, pulled the gag from my mouth, and grinned.

The old Irish guy said: "People were wondering why there was no doorman this morning."

"I bet they were," I said.

"This is a posh building," said the old Irish guy. "There is always a doorman. Day and night."

"Yes," I said.

"Especially very early in the morning. The people are used to someone being there when they leave the building."

"Yes," I said.

I asked: "Has this happened before?"

"Yes," said the old Irish guy. "It happens a lot. It's part of the job."

"Only at night?" I asked.

"Mostly at night," said the old Irish guy. "But it also happens during the day."

"Has it happened to you yet?"

"A couple of times," said the old Irish guy.

"Did you know that the doorman in the building next door was killed not long ago?"

"No," I said.

"It was in the newspaper," said the old Irish guy.

"I see," I said.

"A detailed report," said the old Irish guy. "There was even a photo."

"What kind of photo was it?"

"A doorman without a head," said the old Irish guy.

"Without a head?"

"Yes," said the old Irish guy.

The job really wasn't too bad. I carried on working the night shift, the Irish guy worked the day shift. A Sicilian guy worked the third shift from four until twelve.

Once the Sicilian said to me: "Bronsky. Wanna earn some money on the side?"

"Sure," I said.

"An old consul lives here in this building. He's paralyzed and sits in a wheelchair. How would you feel about pushing him to the bank every day? At nine o'clock sharp."

"Okay," I said.

"My wife used to do it," said the Sicilian, "a strong woman, but she's into her ninth month now."

"Okay," I said.

"The old consul pays three dollars for the job. Three dollars per day."

"Okay," I said.

At eight o'clock in the morning my shift was over. I changed, walked around the corner, then two blocks further to 55th Street where Bickford's fast food restaurant was, sat at the bar, ordered a proper breakfast, ate two eggs with ham, toast, and butter, drank three cups of coffee to stay alert, smoked a few cigarettes, and then went back, shortly before nine, to the building on Park Avenue.

The old consul was an odd character. He didn't say a single word to me. When I rang upstairs at his apartment, the door was opened from the inside. An old woman with a stick pushed the consul, who was sitting in his chair, out into the hallway. I introduced myself but the consul didn't respond.

I pushed the wheelchair into the elevator. We zoomed down. The Sicilian wasn't there yet. I asked the old Irish guy where the consul's bank was. He told me where to go.

I pushed the consul to his bank on the corner of 58th Street and Madison Avenue. They already knew to expect us. A bank clerk waved to me as I rolled in the consul. He also showed me the appropriate teller window and the girl there that was responsible for the consul.

I waited a bit on the side until the old consul had been served by the girl at the teller window. I saw him present his savings book, observed how the girl worked the calculating machine and paid out the money to the consul. In America you don't go to the cashier. Everything is taken care of by the girl at the teller window.

I asked one of the bank clerks why the old consul had to come to the bank every day with his savings book, and they told me that it was just a hobby.

Then I rolled the old consul out to the street again. I brought him home safely and received my three dollars from the old woman with the stick.

A few times I tried to start a conversation with the consul but never received a response. The woman with the stick didn't respond when I spoke to her either.

I asked the Sicilian if he knew in which country the consul had worked, but he didn't. The Irish doorman didn't have a clue either. Only once did the Irish doorman, who had known the consul for years, mention that the consul had spoken German frequently, even though he was a true-blue American.

"Whom did the consul speak German to?" I asked.

The Irish doorman said: "To the woman with the wooden leg."

That's when my suspicions first arose. Maybe, I said to myself, the consul was in Berlin. Maybe even in 1939. Maybe – and this is also just a guess – he was not just consul but Consul General!

When I picked up the consul the next day and rolled him across the street, I was almost certain that the man who was sitting before me was none other than the AMERICAN CONSUL GENERAL!

Bronsky, I said to myself. A little accident at the intersection wouldn't hurt! You will push the wheelchair across the curb by mistake … a lightning-fast movement … a passing car … and it's already done.

Bronsky! You must kill the Consul General!

13.

Made an entry in my diary. I wrote: I, Jakob Bronsky, did not kill the American Consul General. Then added: My job as a night doorman ended today. My three weeks as a vacation replacement are over. Have enough money now to finally start the Sixth Chapter and, of course, finish it, perhaps also the Seventh, if my savings aren't depleted before then.

Since I paid off my back rent, the landlady has been friendly and accommodating. Today she said to me: "Mr. Bronsky. The spots on your bed sheet won't come out anymore. I threw out the sheet but you don't have to pay for it."

"Mr. Bronsky! Someone called this morning. I said that you were still asleep."

"That must have been a mistake. No one calls me."

"But someone did, Mr. Bronsky. A relative of yours. I'm afraid I forgot his name."

"I know who that is."

"You should call them back!"

"Thank you. I will."

"Is that an uncle of yours?"

"No. The American brother-in-law of my aunt who was gassed in Europe."

"A distant relative?"

"That's right."

"An American Jew?"

"No. But one who has been here for thirty years."

"He said that he lives in Brooklyn. In a very seedy area. He must be a poor wretch?"

"Quite the opposite. He's stinking rich."

I called my rich relative in Brooklyn.

"This is Jakob Bronsky."

"Good day, Jakob. Nice of you to call."

"Did something happen?"

"Like what?"

"Did someone die or get married?"

"No. Just a family gathering."

"That's what I mean. It can only be for a wedding or a funeral."

"Well, in this case it's neither."

"What's going on?"

"We're moving. Into our new house on Long Island. A small house-warming party. Are you coming?"

"Okay."

"We'll send you a card with the new address."

"That will be nice."

"The party will be next Saturday."

"Okay. Saturday."

I went although I wasn't in the mood for it. I had only seen my relatives once – when I arrived here – and then never again. They didn't interest me, and the feeling was mutual. What did they want from me?

Bronsky! They want to show you their new house. That's all. They want to show you that they've made it. That they have kids, a house and a yard, a new car, a regular and considerable income. That the man of the house isn't a jackoff: He doesn't need to do that. That they speak English, at home, too, and not German. That they have never heard of Warren Street! That they don't give a shit about you – you, Jakob Bronsky, the man they feared when he arrived here, in New York harbor without a cent to his name, because they believed he wanted something from them. But he didn't want a thing.

It seemed as if my relatives really were happy to spend time with me. I said that I found the house nice, the tasteless furniture tasteful, the TV fantastic, the pictures not authentic but modern, the car incredibly classy, the rug in the living room unique, the washing machine very practical; remarked that the teenagers had grown a lot, that the dog was still the same as always. I shook many hands, recognized distant relatives, as well as two genuine cousins.

Someone greeted me whom I had never seen before.

"Are you really a Bronsky?"

"I am indeed."

"I knew the Bronskys in Halle."

"I can't remember."

"In 1926."

"That's when I was born."

"I see.

I thought that the Bronskys didn't survive the war in Europe."

"They did survive it."

"Your parents, too?"

"Yes, that's correct."

"That sounds like a miracle."

"Indeed."

"How did you survive the war?"

"I can't tell you."

"Are your parents here today?"

"No."

"Where are they?"

"They drove to California."

"For good?"

"I don't know."

"Do you regularly get mail? From your parents?"

"Very rarely."

"How come?"

"We don't have anything left to say to each other."

"I don't understand."

"Me neither."

"Are you married?"

"No."

"Why?"

"I don't know."

"But surely you have a secure job?"

"I have no job at all."

"Really?"

"Yes, it's true."

"Is that why your parents are angry with you? Because you aren't married and don't have a job?"

"Perhaps."

"How are your parents doing financially?"

"They're getting by."

"What does your father do?"

"He works as a packer with a large company."

"And your mother?"

"She works in a factory."

"That's too bad."

"Why do you think that's too bad?"

"Because your father used to be a rich businessman."

"That was then."

"And your mother a lady.

I remember: 1926. Your mother was eight months pregnant. Probably with you. What is your first name?"

"Jakob."

"That's right. Jakob. I remember. Your mother said: 'If it's a boy, then his name will be Jakob.'

A real lady, your mother. Back then. Despite her condition. I remember: She was looking for a new servant. Do you remember?"

I said: "That was before I was born."

There was plenty to eat. They were also not stingy with the drinks. Some people critically examined my Parisian suit. Someone asked: "Do you still have that from over there?" – I said: "Yes, I do."

One of my genuine cousins, whom I had only ever seen once, introduced me to a young lady: "This is my cousin Jakob, an aspiring writer. Hasn't been in the country for long. – And this is my friend Joan, a personal secretary."

We drank a whisky soda. My cousin was very tactful and left us alone. I would have liked to tell the personal secretary that I recently fucked a personal secretary in the ass, but I didn't have the courage to tell her.

"Your cousin just told me that you once worked as a delivery boy on Madison Avenue. Is that true?"

"That's true."

"She said you called her once and told her that."

"That's true."
"But people don't usually talk about that sort of thing."

"Why not?"
"Because it isn't proper."
"You think so?"
"People don't talk about those things.
I also work on Madison Avenue."
"Where?"
"Guess!"
"For a publisher?"
"No. For an advertising company.

Are you really a writer?"
"Yes, I'm a writer."
"Your cousin told me that you haven't published anything."
"Not yet."
"That's too bad."
"Yes. I think so, too."

"Will you publish something sometime?"
"I hope so."
"And if you don't succeed?"
"Then that's tough luck."
"Then your work would be for nothing. Just a waste of time."
"Perhaps."

"Do you really write in a foreign language?"

"Yes. I write in German."
"A difficult language?"
"Yes. Pretty difficult."

"What are your biggest problems?"
"Money problems."
"The usual?"
"Yes. The usual."

"Are you dependent on your mother?"
"Why do you ask that?"
"Everyone is dependent on their mother."
"Perhaps."

"You know, I'm interested in psychology."
"Really?"
"Yes. You, too?"
"No."
"How come?"
"I don't know."
"These days everyone is interested in psychology."
"I didn't know that."

"Did you go to college?"
"No."
"Why not?"
"I don't know. The war, I guess."
"There's still time to go."

"I don't feel like doing that."

"Do you have any other problems?"
"No."
"I envy you."
"What do you mean?"
"No emotional problems?"
"No."
"Everyone has emotional problems."
"I don't."

"Have you ever heard of Freud?"
"Never."
"I don't believe you."
"Why?"
"Everyone has heard of Freud."
"But I haven't."
"You're making fun of me!"
"I certainly am not."
"Yes, you are. You're making fun of me."

She walked away, offended. I followed her and met her at the bar. Because I really wanted to fuck her today, I tried to make up. I said: "What I said about Freud was just a joke. I read Freud attentively."
"I thought so."
I said: "Adler and Jung, too."
"Really?"
"Yes."

"I don't know them."
"That doesn't matter."
"And how about your emotional problems?"
"That was only a joke, too."
"You have emotional problems?"
I said: "Everyone has emotional problems."

After the party she gave me a ride. In her car. There she sat, at the steering wheel, with her empty face, not exactly my type, but good enough for a quick fuck: blonde, pretty well built, about my age. I could almost read her thoughts while we drove, for a while without speaking, on the dark highway to Manhattan: What am I doing with this bum! I will drop him off somewhere, on fifty-ninth, midtown, somewhere.

I said: "You know, it's not easy to write in a language that no one wants to speak to me in."

"No one?"

"With the exception of the few emigrants I happen to know."

"Oh, I see."

"That's one of my biggest problems."

"You're talking about the German language?"

"Yes."

"Why don't you write in English then, a language that everyone understands?"

"That won't work."

"You feel an attachment to the German language?"

"Yes."

"I don't get it."

"I don't either."
"Aren't you Jewish?"
"Of course."
"There you have it."

I was right. She let me out of the car midtown.
"Is it far to your place?"
"No."
"The subway runs all night."
"I know."

14.

The summer had been especially hot. Those who could afford it fled the city. The air conditioning was on full blast in the emigrants' cafeteria. But after midnight, as usual, it was turned off and the hot breath of the city forced its way through the open entrance door.

I didn't worry about the heat; worked doggedly, keeping to schedule, night after night, drank a ton of coffee, and smoked the usual number of cigarettes. THE JACKOFF was coming along nicely. When I had finished the Seventh Chapter, I still had ten dollars.

I thus said to myself: Bronsky. You actually finished writing not just the Sixth Chapter but the Seventh Chapter, too, and you still have ten bucks in your pocket. You now have to make a decision: Continue – start the Eighth Chapter – or look for a job?

I had decided to look for a job. Around one in the afternoon I went to Warren Street, by bus, but this time as a paying passenger.

To my astonishment, I saw that Micky Silberstein's office was closed. A huge sign hung at the door: CLOSED DUE TO BEREAVEMENT!

Bad luck, I thought. Damned bad luck. Who might have died? Was Micky Silberstein married? Did his wife die, or his mother, his father, or someone else in the family? I walked on, shaking my head, down the long hallway, past the many agencies. I saw many notes on the doors of the agencies but the jobs they offered didn't interest me. On the last door, at the end of the hallway, an extra large poster caught my attention: YOUNG WAITER WANTED! CATSKILL MOUNTAINS! GREAT JOB FOR THREE-DAY WEEKEND! 150 DOLLARS GUARANTEED! STUDENTS ONLY!

Of course, I went right inside. Behind the desk sat a fat Irish guy, a typical anti-Semite. He grinned when he saw me.

"What kind of a job is it?" I asked.

"It's in the Catskill Mountains," said the Irish guy. "Do you know what the Catskill Mountains are?"

"No," I said, although I knew it well.

"They're the Jewish mountains close to New York. Why don't you know that?"

"I just didn't know."

"The job isn't for you, boy."

"Why is it not for me?"

"Because you're too old, boy. Didn't you see the poster? It says on there: Young waiter wanted!"

"But I'm not old."

"Yes, you are. For that job you're too old."

"I don't understand." The fat Irish guy laughed. "I'm telling you that you're too old, boy. It's a posh hotel in the Catskill Mountains. That's where the rich Jewish broads go to fuck the young waiters. They only want a student, do you understand? A young one!"

"I could say I'm a student?"

"But you don't look like it, boy. I can't send you there. The boss told me: He must be young and a student."

"Then your boss can kiss my ass."

"Okay, boy," said the fat Irish guy.

I was in a pretty bad mood when I found myself back out in the hallway. I didn't feel like carrying on looking for work, so I left the building. Outside on the street, I looked around. I knew that a bit further up, at the street corner, there was a little cafeteria – run-down, dirty, smeared, unwashed windows – the well-known Warren Street Cafeteria where the bums who hadn't found a job sat around. That's where I wanted to go to drink a cup of coffee.

At the table next to me sat a bum who caught my eye. He wore a worn-out, spotty tuxedo that looked as if its owner had slept in it for several nights, maybe somewhere in the Bowery, the neighborhood where New York's bums and drunks congregated, or on a park bench. I saw the neck of a whisky bottle sticking out of the left tuxedo pocket. The man wore a shirt that used to be white but was now completely filthy. Something in his old, eaten-away face told me that this was a man who knew life inside and out; who knew the game, but who didn't care. Probably someone, I said to myself, who had been finished off by the bottle.

The man sat at a table alone, just like me. At one point he got up to get a roll of bread. When he returned, his table had been occupied by other bums. The man looked around and then came to my table.

"Is there a free seat here?"

"Yes."

We immediately started talking.

"So, buddy, are you a waiter, too?"

"Yes. Occasionally."

"I can tell by your black pants."

"Yes."

"I also work occasionally as a waiter. That's why I'm wearing my tuxedo. Put it on right away this morning to make a better impression at the agency."

"Yes. I can see that."

I told him what had happened with the job in the Catskill Mountains.

"You had bad luck, boy. It's just that you aren't twenty anymore."

I said: "Yes."

"And not a student."

"Yes."

"Bad luck, boy."

I said: "Yes.

Anyhow, what's it like in those posh Jewish hotels in the Catskill Mountains? Is it true that the women go there to fuck the young waiters?"

"That's true, boy."

"How does it work?"

"It's very simple, boy. These women's husbands have to work hard to provide a nice and comfortable life for their wives and to send their kids to college later. That's how it is. They work the whole shitty summer long. Some work overtime or have two jobs. They stay in New York, you see? But they want to get rid of their wives for a while. And the kids, too. And so, during the intense heat, they send them to a spa hotel in the Catskill Mountains. So that they get some fresh air and a bit of distraction."

"And do the husbands know that their wives fuck the waiters there in the spa hotels?"

"They know but pretend not to."

"And why do these waiters have to be students?"

"Because the female guests at those kind of spa hotels wouldn't fuck an ordinary waiter."

"Are there enough students for all the spa hotels in the Catskill Mountains?"

"More than enough," said the bum in the tuxedo. "Thousands of New York students work as waiters in the spa hotels during the summer break to make money for tuition. And the women know that and that's why they go there. And the bosses know that, too; I mean they know why the women go there, and they're okay with it because it's good business."

"Why do the women only want young students? After all, aren't there students who are a bit older?"

"They only want the really young ones."

"Does it have something to do with the cult of youth in this country?"

"It does."

"And why can't one of these waiters be an unknown writer, let's say, one with a good cock? Why do the bosses only want a student? An unknown writer is, after all, not just some common waiter: The women can happily go ahead and fuck him."

"The bosses don't want an unknown writer," said the bum in the tuxedo. "Either because he's not young enough or because an unknown writer counts as a bum. And these women want nothing to do with bums. The bosses know that, too."

"And how about the students?"

"A student isn't a bum," said the bum in the tuxedo. "A student is someone these women respect because he will most likely amount to something at some point."

"I see."

"Besides, hiring students is a trend in spa hotels. And you can't do anything about trends in America. Those damned spa hotels are just places to fuck students. That's how it is. And no one can change it."

"And how is it in the non-Jewish spa hotels?"

"The same, boy. The same. But no one talks about those, at least not in New York."

"Why?"

"Because people in New York only talk about the Catskill Mountains, which are close by."

"Where are the non-Jewish spa hotels? Are there none close to New York?"

"There are a few but they're unsuitable. Most of them are far away, in Palm Beach, at Lake George, and in the Adirondack Mountains."

"Have you ever been there?"

"I worked as an assistant chef in one of the spa hotels there."

"Where was that?"

"At Lake George."

"A non-Jewish hotel?"

"Yes. A non-Jewish hotel. No Jew dared to go in because only Wasps stayed there."

"What are 'Wasps'?"

"People of pure English descent. 'Wasp' is an abbreviation for white Anglo-Saxon Protestant."

"I didn't know that."

"You haven't been here long, have you?"

"No, not long."

"It was even worse at this Wasp hotel, where I once worked as an assistant chef, than at the Jewish spa hotels in the Catskill Mountains. There the women of pure English-Protestant descent even fucked the student waiters outdoors, at night, of course, around the swimming pool, on the lounge chairs, or on the soft rubber mats."

"How wonderful."

"Yes. Indeed.

See, boy," said the old bum in the tuxedo. "In New York you don't have a chance with those classy broads. Either due to a lack of opportunity or because they are married and faithful to their husbands when they're not on vacation, or because they are so expensive that the mere thought of having to spend so much dough takes your breath away even before the first date. But at one of those spa hotels, it's a totally different story."

"How come?"

"Because the American woman generally abandons her principles when she's on vacation."

"I didn't know that."

"But that's how it is. You can't change it."

"Yes," I said.

"Many of these women go to the Catskill Mountains, many a bit further, but some travel to Europe. The musclemen on the Mediterranean beaches could tell you a thing or two about that."

"How do you know all of this?"

"Because I've gotten around a lot."

"I can imagine that."

"Yes," said the old bum in the tuxedo.

I got myself another coffee, sat down again, and looked at my cheap watch. I said: "As a matter of fact, I need a job."

"Have you been around all the agencies?"

"Not all," I said. "I was only on the first floor."

"I'll show you where you can get a job," said the old bum.

"Okay," I said.

The old bum went back with me to No. 80 Warren Street. I followed him up to the third floor. Saw right away what was going on.

In front of one of the agencies stood a line of men. I saw the large poster on the door: 20 WAITERS WANTED URGENTLY FOR TONIGHT! 3 DOLLAR FEE! AGE UNIMPORTANT! TUXEDO REQUIRED!

"So, what do you say?" said the old bum in the tuxedo. "I already saw the poster an hour ago."

"Why didn't you take the job? You have a tuxedo!"

"Because the job costs three dollars. And I don't have three dollars."

"Bad luck for you," I said.

"Yes," said the old bum in the tuxedo.

I said: "The job isn't for me either. I have three dollars but I don't have a tuxedo."

"Bad luck for you," said the old bum.

"Yes," I said. "Bad luck for me."

"The job isn't in Manhattan," said the old bum in the tuxedo. "I already inquired. Earlier. I also know the restaurant. Long way there. Great Neck City. But the job is good. Three hundred bucks."

"That kind of job doesn't exist. There isn't anywhere you can earn three hundred bucks in one night."

"Yes, there is," said the old bum in the tuxedo. "You can't earn it honestly. But if you're smart, then you can earn it."

"Three hundred bucks?"

"Three hundred bucks.

Listen up, boy," said the old bum in the tuxedo. "I'll make you a suggestion. I have a tuxedo but not three dollars. For you it's the opposite. You've got three dollars but no tuxedo. True?"

"True," I said.

"How about we help each other out?"

"What do you mean?"

"You lend me three dollars. And I'll lend you a tuxedo."

"Do you have a second tuxedo?"

"I still have an old one from the days when I worked as a waiter."

"Where?"

"At home."

"I don't think you have a home."

"Not at my actual home," said the old bum in the tuxedo. "I have the tuxedo in a suitcase."

"Where's the suitcase?"

"In a basement. In an old house in the Bowery. Where I'm sleeping at the moment."

"We'll see," I said.

"You won't regret it," said the old bum in the tuxedo. "I'll show you the trick for earning three hundred bucks. You have my word."

"Okay," I said.

"Listen up, boy," said the old bum in the tuxedo. "When you walk into the agency, don't tell the guy behind the desk your name. Think of a false name. Don't show him your Social Security number either."

"Okay," I said.

We walked into the agency. I saw a lot of bums there, too, but no one seemed to own a tuxedo. The job was definitely still up for grabs. Behind the desk sat a guy with the face of a crook. It's all the same to him, I thought. He only wants your three dollars. You can tell him whatever you like.

"What's your name?" asked the guy with the face of a crook.

"Robert McCormick," I said.

"You don't look like someone who could be called McCormick," said the guy with the face of a crook.

I asked: "What do I look like?"

"Like someone who could be called Fischbein or Cohn."

"Fischbein," I said.

"So, Fischbein?"

"Yes," I said. "Fischbein."

"Do you have a Social Security number?"

"I forgot it at home."

"Don't want to pay your taxes, eh?"

"I forgot it at home."

"Okay, Fischbein," said the guy with the face of a crook. "And how about a tuxedo?"

"I forgot that at home, too."

"There's no point in lying to me," said the guy with the face of a crook, "because you can't work there without a tuxedo. If you arrive there without a tuxedo, they'll send you away again immediately."

"But I do have a tuxedo."

"Okay, Fischbein," said the guy with the face of a crook. "Now give me the three dollars."

I gave him the money and he wrote something on a piece of paper, stamped it with the company seal, and gave me the scrap of paper. I read: Fischbein, waiter, work for one day. Then there was the address of the restaurant in Great Neck City.

The guy with the face of a crook said: "Next!"

My new friend, the old bum in the tuxedo, told the guy with the face of a crook a similar story. I quickly handed him three dollars. He paid and got his scrap of paper.

We walked to the Bowery.

"I told the guy that my name is Fischbein."

"I heard that."

"And you?"

"I said my name is Eisenhower."

"Like our president?"

"Exactly."

"Is Eisenhower your real name?"

"Of course not.

It doesn't matter what my real name is," said the old bum in the tuxedo. "People call me Pinky."

"Okay, Pinky," I said.

"And what do they call you?"

"Bronsky."

"Are you really called Bronsky?"

"Yes. I'm called Bronsky."

15.

Pinky lived for free in the basement of a condemned building that had already been half torn down. The rats ran around in the basement. It reeked of death, decay, and trash. Next to old, broken washing machines there was lots of junk, among it Pinky's suitcase with the tuxedo.

"Say, where do you sleep? In between the washing machines?"

"No. There's a back exit with a stairway that's protected from the wind."

Pinky took the tuxedo out of the shabby suitcase. It was in horrible condition.

"Put it on now," said Pinky, "to give it a bit of shape."

"I think it's too large."

"That doesn't matter," said Pinky.

"You have to lend me another dollar," said Pinky, "so that I can buy a clean shirt."

"You can't get a shirt for one dollar."

"Yes, I can," said Pinky. "I know a store close by where they have white nylon shirts. For one dollar."

We bought the shirt for Pinky. Then we went to the train station. "Can you buy me a ticket, too?" asked Pinky.

"Okay," I said.

On the train to Great Neck City, Pinky said: "I know the place where we're going to work tonight. That's also why I know that the job is worth three hundred bucks."

"How do you know the place?"

"I looked at it once. A few months ago."

"Why?"

"Because the place is well known among bums who have been in this 'business' for many years, and because word got around about the three hundred bucks. I wanted to see if it's true."

"Is it true?"

"It's true."

"What kind of place is it?"

"The largest dance place in Great Neck City."

"And what's the deal with the three hundred bucks?"

"I'll explain in a minute.

Listen up, Bronsky boy," said Pinky. "Here's the deal: It's a huge fricking place. Around two hundred tables. A stage with a band – one of those proper fricking music bands with all the bells and whistles. A bunch of waiters. They never have enough. That's why they needed twenty extra to help out tonight. That's the deal, Bronsky boy. That's it. There's also a head waiter and a couple of pretty broads who act as hostesses, as well as a few overseers and bouncers."

"And how do you plan to make three hundred bucks in a place

like that?"

"I'll explain in a minute.

Listen up, Bronsky boy," said Pinky. "Here's the deal: In this fricking place none of the guests pay at the checkout register, as is common everywhere else. Here the waiter collects the money, got it?"

"Got it."

"Of course, the boss knows exactly how much each waiter collects because you can't carry anything out of the kitchen or the bar, neither food nor drinks, without leaving a receipt. Do you know what a receipt is?"

"Yes," I said.

"Okay," said Pinky. "You get a bunch of empty receipts from the head waiter. Every time you carry something out of the kitchen, or out of the bar, you hand in a receipt, write your name on it, your waiter number, and the price of the respective food and drinks. Then the boss knows exactly what you have to collect. Got it?"

"Got it."

"You take in at least three hundred dollars in such a lousy outfit. That's for sure. Around four in the morning, when the place closes, the accounts are settled. You give the money to the boss and get your percentage."

"No tips?"

"Not in this dance establishment. They work with percentages. Ten percent. Not much. But the revenue makes the difference. The waiters know it. The guests know it. And the boss knows it."

"And how do you make three hundred bucks there?"

"I'll explain that in a minute.

Listen up, Bronsky boy," said Pinky. "Here's the deal: We don't wait until four in the morning when the place closes. We collect what is ours and beat it before the boss starts to cash up as usual and settles up with the waiters. We beat it an hour earlier. Something like that."

"Understood."

"We can, of course, make more than three hundred bucks. But it's difficult to say in advance. In any case, it'll be a nice wad of money."

"And if they catch us?"

"No one will catch us."

"Can you be so sure?"

"Absolutely.

Listen up, Bronsky boy," said Pinky. "Here's the deal: The police have more important things to worry about than to scour eight million New Yorkers for two waiters called Fischbein and Eisenhower, especially for such a bagatelle. The police really do have bigger fish to fry. Have you seen the papers?"

"Yes," I said.

"You see?" said Pinky.

"Actually, you're right."

"What's more," said Pinky, "this lousy outfit belongs to a mafia clique. And, as everyone knows, they don't go to the police. No need to worry."

"But they could track us down?"

"They don't have time for that. It's not worth it for just a few bucks. They don't waste their time on things like that. They make million-dollar business deals. But you can't show yourself in that place again. That's all."

"And what about No. 80 Warren Street? We can't go there again either?"

"Yes," said Pinky.

"You can still go there. Only I'd avoid the agency on the third floor if I were you. The one that gave you the job."

The neck of Pinky's whisky bottle still stuck out of the right pocket of his tuxedo. When the first houses of Great Neck City appeared, Pinky grabbed the bottle, drank until it was empty, grinned at me, and rolled the bottle under his seat.

It was shortly before five when we arrived at the train station of Great Neck City. The job was supposed to start at five. At least that's what it said on the work note that the agency had given us. Still, we did not hurry. Pinky knew exactly where the place was. We walked slowly, talked, and smoked. Pinky had put his new shirt on straightaway and carried the old one, wrapped in newspaper, under his arm. Because I had already slipped into the old, wrinkled, and rather dirty tuxedo in Pinky's rat-infested basement, I also carried my black pants that I had worn before under my arm, not wrapped in newspaper but in a plastic bag that I had found between the washing machines in Pinky's pigsty of a dwelling.

It wasn't far to the dance hall. In front of the large entryway stood a small, pockmarked doorman in a blue livery. We asked him where the office was, and he told us.

A typical Mafia joint. The boss and a few other Mafiosi with mask-like faces were in a small office – they sat there stiffly in their expensive suits and stared at us angrily when we entered in our dirty tuxedos. We showed our work notes. The boss didn't deign to speak to us. He said something in Italian to the other Mafiosi – they merely nodded – then he phoned the head waiter who came right away.

"Who sent these bums?" asked the boss.

"The agency," said the head waiter.

"These fellas haven't washed for at least a year," said the boss. "If we allow such waiters to work here, we'll soon have to close the place up."

"I told the agency not to send us any bums," said the head waiter.

"Send these two home," said the boss.

"We can't do that," said the head waiter. "We need every man tonight."

I saw that the boss was getting red in the face. He started to yell: "Get those two outta here!"

"Get out," said the head waiter.

We left and hung around in front of the large entryway for a while. Pinky thought that the head waiter would call us back soon. He was right. The head waiter came out after a few minutes and waved to us. We followed him into the ballroom.

The ballroom was already swarming with waiters who were setting tables. We were clearly a bit late.

"I talked to the boss," said the head waiter. "We really need every man tonight. Go to the kitchen and ask the dishwasher to give you a cleaning rag. Clean your tuxedos with hot water and black coffee."

"Okay," said Pinky.

"Then you go to the office and give the boss your names and

Social Security numbers."

"Okay," said Pinky.

"Then you go to the locker room and leave your clothing there, or whatever it is you have wrapped up in that newspaper and plastic bag."

"Okay," said Pinky.

"And then you come back here and check in with me."

We did as we were told. We cleaned our tuxedos. We went to the office and gave the boss our false names with false addresses and promised to send the Social Security numbers soon in the mail because we had forgotten the cards with the numbers at home and hadn't memorized them. Then we went to the locker room and left what we had brought: my black pants and Pinky's old shirt. A bit later, when we returned to the ballroom, the head waiter said: "Have one of the regular waiters show you how to set the tables. We have our own system here. When you're done setting tables, you go to the kitchen and get some grub. Later you come back to me so that I can give you the receipts for the kitchen and the bar."

"Okay," said Pinky.

"We mostly serve champagne here," said the head waiter. "But people also drink a lot of rye and scotch. Hardly anyone drinks wine here."

"Okay," said Pinky.

"Later I'll also show you what's going on in the kitchen. The menu is straightforward."

"Okay," said Pinky.

"You're dirty," said the head waiter, "but you seem to be

old-timers?"

"Yes, we're old-timers," said Pinky.

After we had found out from the regulars how the tables had to be set, we got to work. Later we went to the kitchen and were given something to eat. The cook, a shady-looking Sicilian with bushy eyebrows and teeth like a horse, gave us a plate of spaghetti with tomato sauce.

"How about some meat?" said Pinky. "In every New York restaurant the waiters get meat."

"You're not in New York here," said the Sicilian cook. "You're in Great Neck City."

Business got started rather late. The first guests came at nine. As long as there wasn't much to do, we took turns going to the bathroom to smoke. Pinky was in a good mood because each of us had been given seven tables and that meant three hundred bucks for sure.

It didn't get busy until eleven. Then there wasn't any time to smoke. The waiters nervously ran back and forth. We did, too. There wasn't much space in between the many tables because the guests stood around chatting and laughing. The waiters literally had to fight their way to the kitchen and bar. A real grind.

Especially for Jakob Bronsky who wasn't very nimble and stumbled frequently with his tray, Jakob Bronsky, who was a poet and not a juggler. Of course, Pinky, the old-timer, was nimbler, and Pinky nodded encouragingly to him. His wise drunkard eyes were already glowing in anticipation of his three hundred bucks.

Shortly after two in the morning, Pinky gave me a sign. I was totally exhausted and drenched in sweat. We collected our money and then I followed Pinky to the men's room. There we counted our dough.

"How much do you have?" asked Pinky.

"Not quite 300. Only 280."

"That's not bad," said Pinky. "280 is almost 300."

"Yes," I said.

"And that's really not bad," said Pinky.

"And how much do you have?"

"A bit more."

"How much?"

"320."

"What do we do now?"

"We beat it."

"Okay. But what about our things? We still have stuff in the locker room. My black pants and your old shirt."

"We can't go to the locker room now."

"Why?"

"They mustn't catch us in the locker room with so much money. That's too suspicious."

"What do we do?"

"We can't go out through the back door either because the guard will see us there."

"And how about the front exit?"

"The bouncers are there, as well as the doorman."

"What do we do?"

"We go through the kitchen. There's an exit next to the dishwasher that leads to the trash cans."

"Isn't that suspicious?"

"The kitchen isn't suspicious. Neither is the kitchen exit because the waiters often step out for some fresh air whenever there's a moment where they have nothing to do."

"And what about our things? In the locker room?"

"Forget them."

It all went as planned. You could rely on Pinky. We slipped out through the kitchen, went around the trash cans in the yard, and stepped through a gate into the dark street. Once outside, we started to run.

I shouted to Pinky: "Are we running to the train station?"

"No," shouted Pinky, panting. "It'll take too long until the train gets here. We'll run to the next taxi stand."

16.

We met again one more time – Pinky and I – in the little cafeteria where the bums congregated, at the corner of Warren Street. I returned his tuxedo, freshly cleaned.

"What are you going to do now, Pinky?"

"Don't know yet."

"Will you rent an apartment?"

"No, boy. I need the money for more important matters."

"Whisky?"

Pinky nodded. "I've already bought two cases and hidden them between the washers."

"But you're not drunk today?"

"I'll try to stay sober for a while. But I know that it won't work for long."

"When will you start drinking again?"

"Don't know yet.

And what will you do with the money?"

"I will write, Pinky."

"What are you writing, boy?"

"A book."

"How long can you live off the money?"

I said: "Maybe two months."

"But then you'll have to use it sparingly."

"I've learned how to manage."

"You think we'll maybe meet again?"

"Maybe," I said.

"At No. 80 Warren Street. When we're looking for work again?"

"Maybe," I said.

We sat together for a while longer and talked about the jobs we'd had. Later I accompanied Pinky to the Bowery, where I took the subway.

The money was supposed to last two months so I could finish writing the biggest chunk of my future bestseller, THE JACKOFF. I lived frugally, pinched every lousy cent, cut my cigarettes in half, skimped on eggs at breakfast, even on the toast; although I took my own coffee, I mixed in some of Mr. Selig's, ate mostly just soup or whatever dishes were being sold cheapest at the cafeteria. But I still ended up spending more money than planned. Sometimes I went to the movies because I needed distraction or got a street whore when the cold showers no longer helped.

Once, at a Times Square theater, I sat next to a young Negro. I had never seen a man stare at the screen with such fascination. The Negro was extremely restless. He constantly twitched his head and swung his knees. When Doris Day showed a bit too much of her legs, the Negro opened his fly. Maybe he thought of all the white women he wanted to have but couldn't get … at least not now: not in 1953. I saw how he took his black cock out and unashamedly started to masturbate. For a while I watched, then I felt like smoking, stood up, and went upstairs, into the smokers' lounge.

One Saturday I decided to go to a dance hall. I had just finished the Tenth Chapter and thought that a creative break couldn't hurt. Of course, I also hoped to meet a girl.

First, I went to the Roseland but had no success. I left the dance hall around midnight and tried it at the "friendship club over 28", the ball for lonely hearts.

There they could also tell that I had no dough. Something wasn't right with me; the women noticed it right away. I said to myself: Bronsky. The youngest women here are at least forty. But the forty-year-olds are all stuck-up because they're younger than the others. You don't stand a chance. If you want to be sure, then you'd best try it with an old one. Maybe it'll work.

I danced with a woman who was about 65. Said to myself: A hole's a hole. Beggars can't be choosers. And when you go to bed with her tonight, tell her not to take her teeth out. It'll work out. You're sure to get it up. And you need it badly, damn it.

The woman wasn't so bad. Her figure was all right. Her legs, too. She pressed her old tits against my Parisian suit during the slow foxtrot. At one point, I kissed her on her wrinkled neck.

I invited her to a drink. She asked me if I had a job. I said: "Yes. And a good one at that."

The old woman told me that she lived on Coney Island and asked me if I wanted to take her home in my car. When I told her that I hadn't brought my car tonight, she just left. I went home and took a cold shower.

After finishing two more chapters, my cock was so hard that I thought I was going to go crazy. Still, I didn't want to jack off or go to a street whore. I spontaneously decided to call a marriage broker.

Because I needed help urgently, I got an appointment right away. By early afternoon, I was sitting in the marriage broker's office.

"I see that you haven't been here long," said the marriage broker. "A greenhorn, eh?"

"Yes," I said.

"Many of the new immigrants want to get married," said the marriage broker. "That is sensible."

"Yes," I said.

"It's always for the best," said the marriage broker.

"Yes," I said.

I said: "I would like a girl around 25."

"That's not possible," said the marriage broker.

"Why is that not possible?"

"Because you're too old."

I said: "I'm 27."

"But you look older."

"I know."

"You could be forty."

"I know."

"In America," said the marriage broker, "women want men their own age. That's how it is. It doesn't matter how old you really are."

"What does matter?"

"How old you look.

If you look like you're forty," said the marriage broker, "then no 25-year-old girl will take you. Except if you're a millionaire. That would, of course, be different. Are you a millionaire?"

"No," I said. "I'm not a millionaire."

"I might have a girl for you," said the marriage broker. "Well, she isn't really a girl anymore. She's 38."

"38?"

"Yes, that's right," said the marriage broker. "She's 38 but looks thirty, so ten years younger than you, because you look like you're forty."

"Ten years younger than me?"

"Yes, that's right," said the marriage broker. "Basically, conventional rules state that you don't have a chance. But I could give it a try."

"Okay," I said.

"Do you have a steady income?"

"Yes," I said.

"How much?"

"150 per week."
"That's not bad at all."
"It's fine for me."

"You must never be satisfied with your income," said the marriage broker. "You can tell me but whatever you do, don't tell the girl. A man has to improve himself. He must be determined and aim high. Once you're on the ladder, you have to climb it. Otherwise you're a loser."

"You're very right about that."

"Don't tell the girl that you're a loser."

"I definitely won't."

"So, what's your job?"

"I'm a journalist."

"Which newspaper do you work for?"

"None."

"How can you be a journalist then?"

"I'm freelance."

The marriage broker got a photo album out of his desk, spent a while looking, found the right page, and showed it to me.

"Have a good look at this girl!"

"That's what I'm doing."

"How do you like her?"

"She's not exactly my type."

"Why?"

"A bit too big, I think. And she wears glasses."

"She looks like Elizabeth Taylor," said the marriage broker, "… if Elizabeth Taylor gained weight, wore glasses, and were a few years older."

"Do you really think so?"

"Oh, for sure," said the marriage broker. "You just have to have the right eye."

Under the picture were a few details about this 'girl'. I read: Shirley Schwarz, 38, Jewish, five feet nine, 170 pounds, loves music, theater, movies, and the outdoors. Profession: personal secretary.

Bronsky, I said to myself. You don't want to get married anyway; you just want a quick fuck. She isn't your type but she is a personal secretary, and now you will finally have the opportunity to fuck a real personal secretary.

"An educated girl," said the marriage broker. "Just right for you. She also belongs to the Jewish faith. Like you."

"Yes," I said.

"I do have a lot of other girls on file," said the marriage broker, "… also non-Jewish, Irish girls, and many others … but since there are three million Jews in New York City, I don't see why, as a Jew, you should marry a non-Jew. You know what I mean: I'm not prejudiced but I believe it is better when the children are brought up in the faith of their parents. Then there are no conflicts."

"I have nothing against Irish girls," I said, "or any of the others, and I don't give a shit about religion, and as far as children are concerned, we'll figure something out."

"You don't want the girl?"

"I didn't say that."

"I can show you others."

"That's not necessary."

"What do you actually want?"

"Let me think about it."

I lit a cigarette and thought long and hard.

"I will try this girl," I said, "because she's a personal secretary."

"You see," said the marriage broker. "A personal secretary, that's something!"

"Yes," I said.

"The deal will cost you fifty dollars," said the marriage broker. "If it doesn't work out with the girl, then I'll introduce you to others, and you don't have to pay me a single cent. All for just fifty dollars. Believe me, I am the cheapest marriage broker in New York."

"Right now I only have twenty dollars."

"Then give me the twenty. But I must warn you that if it doesn't work out with this girl, then I won't introduce you to another unless you pay the rest."

"Okay," I said.

"How will I meet the girl? In your office?"

"No," said the marriage broker. "We're not strict about introductions here. You'll get the phone number of the girl, and her address, and you just call her."

"And the girl?"

“She gets your address and your phone number. As well as all your details. I will call her today.”

“Will the girl call me?”

“Of course not. The man must always make the first move. The girl will call from time to time later on, of course, once we’ve gotten things rolling and you two have gotten to know one another.”

“When can I call the girl?”

“Not until tomorrow,” said the marriage broker. “You could also wait a little longer before you call. That makes a better impression.”

I said: “But I’m in a hurry” and thought about my quick fuck.

Before I left, I paid my twenty dollars, left my real name, address, and the phone number of my landlady.

17.

I woke up the next morning with an embarrassing hard-on. Even the cold shower didn't help. Because I was in a hurry and wanted nothing more than to mount my new bride, the personal secretary, right away, I called her immediately after breakfast. A male voice answered.

"Hello?"

I said: "Hello."

"Who are you?"

"Jakob Bronsky."

"Don't know that name."

"I was given this number by the marriage broker."

"Ah, I see."

"And who are you?"

"My name is Schwarz. I'm Shirley's father."

"Does she live with you?"

"Yes. Shirley lives with her parents."

"That's strange."

"Why is that strange?"

"Because young, single people usually live alone."

"What is that supposed to mean?"

"Nothing."

"Shirley lives with us because it's cheaper and because she's saving for a new car. She's also planning a trip around the world."

"Understood."

"Who are you anyway?"

"I already told you. My name is Jakob Bronsky."

"Did the marriage broker send us a picture of you?"

"No."

"Why?"

"Because I didn't give him one."

"You didn't have one on you?"

"Exactly."

"Didn't he request one from you?"

"No. Not from me. He only wanted fifty dollars."

"Listen, young man, my daughter is not at home. She's still at the office. Didn't you know that she works?"

"Yes, I did."

"Why did you call so early then?"

"Because I was in a hurry."

"You don't want to get married tomorrow, do you?"

"No. Certainly not."

"Listen, young man. I don't have time right now. Call in the evening when Shirley is home."

"Okay."

"Do you have a job?"

"Of course."

"What kind of a job?"

"I assume that the marriage broker already told your daughter about it."

"Perhaps."

"Has your daughter really not mentioned anything about me?"

"No."

"But I'm sure the marriage broker has already talked with her."

"Shirley doesn't tell me everything."

"Okay."

"Okay," said the man on the other end of the line.

That evening, when I lifted the receiver and dialed the number of my new bride, my breath quickened. When I heard her voice, I almost came there and then. My hard cock bumped against the telephone cord. I hung up, lit a cigarette, waited until I had calmed down, and dialed the number again. I heard her voice once more.

I said: "This is Jakob Bronsky."

"Didn't you just call?"

"Yes, but the connection was bad."

"My father told me that you already called during the day."

"Yes, shortly after breakfast."

"My father said it was in the afternoon."

"That's right. I always have breakfast late."

"Does that have to do with your work schedule?"

"Exactly."

"So, you are Jakob Bronsky."

"I am Jakob Bronsky."

"And do you know who I am?"

"Of course. You are Miss Schwarz."

"You may call me Shirley."

"Okay, Shirley."

"May I call you Jakob?"

"Of course."

"Mr. Newman has told me a lot about you."

"The marriage broker?"

"I don't like that word."

"Me neither. So, Mr. Newman then."

"Yes. Mr. Newman."

"What did Mr. Newman say about me?"

"He said that you are just right for me."

"That's what he told me, too."

"Really?"

"Yes."

"Are you really a journalist?"

"Yes."

"Which newspaper do you work for?"

"For different ones."

"I regularly read the Herald Tribune. The Times and the News, too, every once in a while, but I have never seen your name."

"I write under a pseudonym."

"Can you reveal it?"

"No."

"Why not?"

"Because there is too much at stake. My articles are very controversial."

"Are your articles political?"

"Yes."

"But you didn't attack the President of the United States, did you?"

"Yes, I did."

"Or Senator McCarthy?"

"The commie crusher?"

"That's the one."

"Of course. Him, too."

"How very interesting."

"Indeed."

"Have you written about the Negro problem, too?"

"That's my main topic."

"And the problem with Puerto Ricans?"

"That, too."

"Tell me about it."

"About the Negroes and Puerto Ricans?"

"Yes."

"I can't think of anything right now."

"But you did write about that, didn't you?"

"Of course. But, you know, once my articles have been printed, I forget about the content."

"But that's strange."

"To shed the ballast. So I can come up with new ideas."

"Ah, I see.

Don't you find it terrible that the Puerto Ricans are having so many children? They're almost like rats."

"They just like to fuck."

"What did you say?"

"I apologize. I didn't mean it that way."

"One should teach them about birth control."

"Yes, that's right."

"Have you written about that, too?"

"Of course."

"The Negroes are also having lots of children but not quite as many as the Puerto Ricans."

"Yes," I said.

"But the Puerto Ricans do have a better family life. At least their kids have a home."

"Yes," I said.

"It's really bad with the Negroes. I feel sorry for the little Negro kids."

"You're right about that."

"And who are the ones who have to pay? For the children, I mean. The taxpayer! Us, Mr. Bronsky. You and me."

"I thought you wanted to call me Jakob."

"Sorry, I mean Jakob. We're the ones who have to pay for the children of Negroes and Puerto Ricans. Isn't that right?"

"You're right," I said.

"Do you pay such high taxes, too?"

"Not really," I said.

"Why?"

"Tax evasion is one of my hobbies."

"You must be joking?"

"Of course," I said.

I lit another cigarette and thought about how my line about tax evasion wasn't a joke. But that wasn't any of her business, same with what I did with my Social Security number and the sort of tricks I used when I had a job.

"Are you still there, Jakob?"

"Yes. I'm still here."

"Mr. Newman told me that you have a regular income of 150 dollars per week."

"Yes, I do."

"Does one have such a regular income as a freelance journalist?"

"Not really. I often earn more. I only gave Mr. Newman my approximate average income but maybe I was a bit too modest."

"So, you actually earn more?"

"Yes."

"Do you like to travel, too?"

"Not really."

"Why?"

"I traveled around so much during the war."

"Oh, I see."

"Yes."

"I'm sorry about that."

"You don't have to be sorry."

"Where did you travel to during the war?"

"I don't like to talk about that."

"Were you also in a concentration camp?"

"I don't like to talk about that."

"You know, I'm planning a trip around the world."

"Your father already told me about it."

"Maybe even to India."

"Really?"

"Yes. Have you been to India?"

"Not yet."

"The people there are supposed to be terribly poor."

"Yes. I've heard that, too."

"Do you go to the theater often?"

"Yes."

"You must surely get free tickets as a journalist?"

"That's right."

"What have you seen?"

"Different things."

"Theater tickets are very expensive. People say the tickets are cheaper in Europe."

"Much cheaper."

"Do you also go to the movies?"

"I do. Often."

"Who is your favorite actor?"

"No one."

"And your favorite actress?"

"Ingrid Bergman."

"Wasn't she involved in a scandal?"

"Yes."

"A pretty bad scandal."

"I don't know about that."

"Do you sometimes have dreams about certain actresses?"

"Sometimes."

"Most men dream about Marilyn Monroe."

"She's not my type."

"You dream about Ingrid Bergman?"

"Correct."

"What happens?"

"I sometimes take her off the screen, at night under my blanket, and fumble around a bit with her."

"You're joking?"

"This time I'm not so sure."

"You don't see her anymore. Usually only in the cheap cinemas where they show old films from time to time. Do you go to cheap cinemas?"

"Sometimes."

"That's not proper."

"Why?"

"Because it isn't."

I could feel my cock rubbing against the telephone cord again. You have to fuck this stupid asshole today! You desperately need a hot cunt. It hurts under your glans, right in that one spot. It's been too long since you've had a woman. You're still young. And you're writing a book. A bit of relaxation will help your writing. You will shoot your semen between the legs of this stupid cow, together with your stress, your loneliness, your longings, your dreams, and your hallucinations. Your head will become clear, your hunger stayed, your thirst quenched.

"How about tonight?" I asked. "We could meet somewhere."

"I'm afraid that's not possible."

"Why?"

"Because today is Friday and I already have a date."

"With a young man?"

"Of course."

"And tomorrow?"

"Tomorrow is Saturday. That is even worse. I have a date tomorrow, too."

"And Sunday?"

"Sunday won't work either."

"You have a date?"

"Yes. I have a date on Sunday, too."

"But I'm lonely," I said, "and I would like to see you tonight."

"Don't you have any female friends?"

"No."

"That's sad."

"Yes."

"Call me again next week. Monday would be best because of my schedule. Maybe we can arrange something for Saturday in two weeks."

"Okay," I said. "We'll speak on Monday." I hung up.

18.

The next day I called the marriage broker with the intention of asking for my twenty dollars back.

"Today is Saturday," said the marriage broker. "How did you know my office was open?"

I said: "Because Saturday is the loneliest day of the week."

"You got that right," said the marriage broker. "On Saturday, the people who don't have a date usually get *katzenjammer.* That's when my phone starts ringing."

"Yes," I said.

"Did you want anything?"

"I want my twenty dollars back."

"No way," said the marriage broker. "Miss Schwarz just called here and told me that she already has a date with you."

"We haven't pinned anything down yet," I said. "I'm supposed to call her again on Monday. It's all taking too long for my liking."

"You just have to be patient," said the marriage broker.

"Patient?"

"Yes," said the marriage broker.

"Miss Schwarz told me everything."

"About what?"

"Your European behavior."

"I don't get what you mean."

"She was disappointed by you but I've put it right now."

"Why was she disappointed?"

"Let me explain.

You don't tell a young lady that you're lonely," said the marriage broker. "You also don't tell her that you don't have any dates because that makes you a loser."

"I didn't think about that."

"You just haven't been in America long enough."

"That's true."

"You also don't ask a lady if she has the intention of meeting you the same night. That's not proper. Or on the next day, which happens to be a Saturday of all days. Or on the day after that, which happens to be a Sunday of all days. You don't do such a thing. You're acting as if you weren't aware that a girl in this country can't admit to not having a date on the weekend. That's not possible. Every successful woman is either married or has a date on the weekend. Do you understand?"

"Yes," I said.

"A successful woman is not lonely, just like a successful man is not lonely."

"Yes," I said.

"Poverty and loneliness are a disgrace in this country."

"Yes," I said.

"If I can give you one piece of advice: Never talk about poverty or loneliness."

"I didn't say anything about poverty."

"But you mentioned loneliness?"

"Yes. That's true."

"Like I said, I've already fixed everything. Miss Schwarz is expecting your call on Monday."

On Monday, I called my new bride again. This time she wanted to know how tall I was, whether I had hair or was bald, whether I looked youthful and fit – the way one has to look to be "in" – whether I had plans for the future, and whether I believed in myself. I answered evasively. But ultimately she agreed to go out on a date with me.

"Well, okay," she said. "On Saturday at seven. Are you inviting me to dinner?"

"Of course."

"To a nice restaurant?"

"Naturally."

"I'm looking forward to it."

"Yes. Me, too."

"Are you picking me up?"

"I'd be delighted to."

"You could ring the doorbell," she said, "but it would be too much trouble because you can't park your car in front of the building."

"Why not?"

"Because there are no parking spots."

"What should I do?"

"I will wait in front of the building for you," she said. "Drive up to the building in your car, stop briefly – that won't be a problem – and

I will get in quickly. That way you won't have any parking issues."

"Okay," I said.

"What does your car look like?"

"Is that really important?"

"Of course. I have to be able to recognize your car!"

"It's red," I said. "A red Jaguar."

"Oh, you drive a Jaguar?"

"Correct."

"A new one?"

"A brand new one."

I was glad that she didn't live in Brooklyn or the Bronx, like most Jewish women whom I had met at the Roseland or at the "ball for lonely hearts". To get to Brooklyn, you often had to ride the subway for more than an hour, and it was almost just as far to the Bronx.

The next Saturday, I picked up my old Parisian suit from the cleaners. As well as a clean, white shirt. I chose the best tie hanging in my closet and polished my worn-out Tom McAnn shoes to a shine. In the afternoon, I went for a walk to kill time until my big date. At six-thirty, I took the subway.

She lived in the eastern part of Manhattan, on 11th Street, not far from 2nd Avenue. I took the subway to Union Square and walked the rest of the way. It started to rain. When I arrived – at seven o'clock sharp – she stood waiting in the entryway.

"Hello, Jakob!"

"Hello, Shirley!"

"It's raining. Step closer. Come into the entryway. You're already all wet."

"It's not that bad."

"Where is the Jaguar?"

"I'm afraid it wouldn't start. Left it in the garage."

"That's too bad."

"Yes."

"What do we do now?"

"I don't know."

"You could call a taxi?"

"Okay."

"Have you reserved a table?"

"Where?"

"At a nice restaurant."

"Not yet. We'll get a table without one."

"But not at a renowned restaurant."

"Don't worry about it."

"Do you want to call a taxi now? I'll wait here in the meantime."

"Yes."

I walked through the rain back toward 2nd Avenue. Bronsky, I said to myself. She doesn't weigh 170 pounds like the marriage broker had noted in his album. She surely weighs a hundred pounds more. I estimate 270. And the picture that the marriage broker showed you is probably from when she was much younger: an old trick. And she's also not 38 but at least 48. And she doesn't look ten years younger either. And she wants to go to a renowned restaurant. And she wants to go by taxi. And surely she'll want to go to a nightclub later because it's Saturday or because it's too early to go home on a Saturday. Damn it, Bronsky. What have you gotten yourself into here? And you can't fuck her tonight either because she's living with her parents. And because she'll refuse to come along to your pad. And she surely won't want to go to a hotel either. You know her type. And anyway, your cock isn't hard anymore. It got all soft and limp when you saw her. Bronsky! Be smart and skedaddle!

I walked to Union Square, took the subway, and got out at Times Square.

At Donald's pub I ordered three hamburgers, ketchup, onions, and a decent serving of potato salad. I had a few glasses of beer with it. By the fourth beer, I had almost completely forgotten about my bride. Shirley Schwarz's flabby face gradually faded away; no longer irritatingly hovered above what was left of my hamburgers and potato salad, or over the edge of the plate, or the beer glasses … it became nothing more than a shapeless fatty stain. I smoked three cigarettes, got a black coffee and a colorful banana split. Then I got up, crossed 42nd Street, and went into one of the cheap movie theaters.

When I came out of the theater shortly after eleven, I was no longer thinking about Shirley Schwarz, or the marriage broker, or the lost twenty dollars. I was rather excited, had a hard cock, and now finally wanted my well-earned fuck.

The street whores around Times Square, especially those on 8th Avenue and 42nd Street, were just as depraved as those on upper Broadway, around the emigrants' cafeteria and the block where I lived. So, I said to myself: Bronsky! It's about time that you fuck something proper. Today you will treat yourself to a high-end whore.

The rain had stopped. My Parisian suit had long dried. Slowly, lost in thought, smoking, a hard-on in my pants, I strolled to 57th Street. There I turned right and went over to the east side of Manhattan.

There they were sitting: the high-end whores. In an expensive bar. Corner of 57th Street and 3rd Avenue. You could stand in front of the display window and stare at them. They were pretty. Well-built. Dressed to the nines. Elegant. Hair done in the latest fashion. There they were sitting: at the bar. Sipping their cocktails. Smiling stiffly. Glancing at the window every now and then. Where I was standing. And others, too.

Bronsky, I said to myself. What are you standing around for? What's the point in staring like a lunatic? Go into the bar. Talk to one of them. Buy her a drink.

I sat on the bar stool next to the tall blonde that I was especially hot for. She had the legs of Mistinguett, the body of Esther Williams, and a face that vaguely reminded me of Ingrid Bergman. Man, Bronsky, I said to myself. This is one classy broad. You've never had one like that before. Forget about Shirley Schwarz and her spongy face, her fat legs, her large ass. She's probably still standing in the entryway, staring like a loon, waiting for your taxi.

"Would you like a drink?" I asked the tall blonde.

We drank two cocktails and talked about the weather. Then she followed me out onto the street.

On the way to her hotel, I noticed that her pimp was following us. But I pretended I hadn't seen him.

The room was elegant. There was even a bathroom.

"It'll cost 25 dollars," said the blonde.

"I didn't know it was that expensive."

"You have to pay up front."

"Okay," I said.

I gave her the 25 dollars and watched her stick the money in her purse. She laid the purse on the carpet. She took off her panties. Nothing else.

"Come on," she said.

I didn't even take the time to turn down the sheets of the bed. That's how hot I was for her. I threw her onto the bed and pounced upon her. I barely had time to open the fly of my Parisian pants – the fly with the old-fashioned buttons – when I came.

I said: "That doesn't count."

"What's that supposed to mean?"

"I came prematurely."

"That's bad luck, boy."

"I didn't even stick it in."

"That's bad luck, boy."

"Let me at it again!"

"That'll cost another 25 dollars."

"I don't have that much."

"Look in your wallet."

"Okay," I said.

I gave her another 25 dollars. This time she undressed. Totally. This time we did it properly.

When she went into the bathroom to wash for the next customer, she took her purse with her. She was careful.

19.

In the weeks that followed, I suffered from a terrible thirst. I didn't know what was wrong with me. The more I drank, the thirstier I got. And yet the summer's peak had already long passed. My acquaintances at the emigrants' cafeteria shook their heads. "You're sick, Mr. Bronsky. Why don't you go to a doctor?"

I was working on my Fifteenth Chapter. My cash reserves were gradually dwindling.

But I still intended to finish the first half of my novel. I didn't want to go to a doctor.

It got worse day by day. I had switched my writing beverage from my usual coffee to Coca Cola. The empty bottles were piling up on my table. I often drank twenty Coca Colas in one night of writing. But the worst was that I constantly felt the urge to pee. That obviously disrupted my writing, because every time I had to get up and go to the bathroom.

I slept badly, woke up every hour, drank tap water, and went to the bathroom. Once I peed the bed. Early in the morning I'd wake up with a heavy head. My limbs felt like lead. I often stayed in bed until it got dark outside. Then I got up, dragged myself wearily to the emigrants' cafeteria, and tried to work on my book, but I couldn't concentrate.

I did go to a doctor though, in the end.

"You have diabetes, Mr. Bronsky!"

"That cannot be?"

"Do you know of any cases in your family?"

"Yes. A few. Both grandmothers had it."

"There you are. It's hereditary.

I have to take a second urine sample," said my doctor. "We also need a blood sample. If your diabetes isn't too severe and there are no complications, I can treat you with pills. Otherwise you'll need injections."

"Insulin?"

"Insulin!"

The blood test results were appalling, as were those of my second urine sample. I didn't just have high blood sugar – higher than the doctor had expected – but my blood was also poisoned: The doctor called it ketoacidosis – a typical complication of serious diabetes that is long neglected and left untreated.

I had to go to hospital. Stayed there for two weeks. My body was detoxified. I received insulin, as well as salt tablets, because my body had lost too much water. The nurses showed me how to inject insulin. It's basically very simple. I was eager to learn. It wasn't long before I could inject myself.

After I had been discharged from the hospital, I bought, with a valid prescription, my own needle that I could sterilize, and a month's supply of insulin. I had to inject daily now, right after getting up, before breakfast. When I ran out of insulin, I went back to my private doctor to give urine and blood samples and to get a new insulin prescription.

The doctor presented me with a bill. I told him flat out that I didn't have the money right now. To my great astonishment, he understood.

"When can you pay, Mr. Bronsky?"

"In approximately four months."

"That's pretty long."

"You see, I'm expecting money. A large sum."

"Maybe you could pay a little sooner?"

"No. There's no way."

"Okay," said the doctor.

"How often do I have to come here?"

"Once a month. For the urine and blood samples, and for your insulin prescription."

"Okay," I said.

My doctor was extremely nice. Perhaps he really believed that I would pay the bill. Perhaps he thought I was someone with a conscience.

"How are you feeling, Mr. Bronsky?"

"I'm feeling considerably better."

"Not thirsty anymore?"

"Not thirsty anymore. I also don't have to pee so much either."

"Are you watching your diet?"

"Of course."

"No candy? No Coca Cola? Fat-free foods?"

"Yes."

"That's very sensible."

"It's just sometimes I get dizzy. Not long ago I fell down on the street."

"That's from the insulin. We call that insulin shock. You probably injected too much or didn't eat regularly enough."

"Perhaps."

"If you get one of those attacks again, just eat a bit of sugar."

"I thought I wasn't supposed to eat sugar?"

"That's right. But when you have an attack, you must eat sugar."

"Isn't that a contradiction?"

"That's just how it is. A diabetic's blood sugar is generally too high but sometimes – due to the insulin – it drops all of a sudden and then it's too low. You get an attack – we call it insulin shock – and you have to eat sugar. That's how it is."

"Will the attack then pass?"

"Usually, yes."

"And if not?"

"Some die during such an attack."

"But I didn't die."

"You were just lucky."

"Doctor. I'm afraid of having these attacks!"

"No need to be afraid. You just have to lead a regular lifestyle, and don't inject too much or too little. Then you won't have any attacks."

"Lead a regular lifestyle, you say?"

"Exactly. Sleep regularly. Eat regularly. Work regularly. No extravagances. No extreme exertion. No stress. No worries. No excitement. The smallest change can mess up a diabetic's metabolism and influence the effect of the insulin."

"And then the attacks happen?"

"That's right."

"Anything else?"

"Or you'll end up in hospital again with more poisoning and high blood sugar."

"I've gotten myself into a fine mess here!"

"You have, indeed."

"Doctor. You know, I'm a writer. Can diabetics still write?"

"You can scribble as much as you want, provided that you are able to concentrate."

"That's what I mean."

"It depends on your lifestyle. If your metabolism works well, which, in turn, is dependent on you leading a regular lifestyle, then you will be able to concentrate."

"But I can't lead a regular lifestyle."

"But you must."

"Doctor. Tell me: How about fucking? Are diabetics still allowed to fuck?"

"You may. Provided that you can, of course."

"How do you mean that?"

"Some diabetics lose their virility."

"Will that be the case for me?"

"I don't know."

The doctor got up and gave me his hand. He smiled sympathetically. I had to go through the waiting room to get to the exit. The patients in the waiting room stared at me and I had the feeling that they were all looking at my cock. Outside, on the street, I had another attack.

I decided to look for work again because I only had a few dollars left in my pocket. Bronsky, I said to myself. Buy yourself some cheap waiter's pants at the junk dealer because you left the old ones in Great Neck City. Take the subway and go to Warren Street. Stop worrying about your cock. The doctor only scared you. Your cock is fine.

The Silberstein agency was open again. Micky Silberstein offered me the usual jobs as a substitute for a few days. I earned what I needed to get by and already started to once again make plans to somehow get money and finish writing the JACKOFF.

I often looked out for Pinky because I thought he knew where we could land another big fish, but Pinky seemed to have disappeared without a trace. He wasn't at Warren Street nor was he in his rat-infested basement. Maybe he had moved out. Once – when I was on my way back to his rat-infested basement, hoping to run into him this time – I noticed that the building didn't exist anymore. It had been torn down.

I was wracked with worry over my hospital bill. It could arrive any day. You could talk to your family doctor but there was no messing around with those in charge at the hospital. I had no health insurance and didn't know what to do. I didn't want to end up in court either.

One night I moved out of my apartment, secretly, three weeks behind on rent. I found a cheap room in a sleazy hotel. Bronsky, I said to myself. Since people don't have to register their address in America, the hospital bill will never reach you.

It didn't really work out with the jobs. Sudden attacks of dizziness often caught me by surprise. Then my knees started trembling, and my hands. Once – when I was working as a sub waiter – I spilled a whole bowl of soup onto a lady's new evening gown. I was fired without notice.

The bosses complained to Micky Silberstein, and Micky Silberstein looked at me sadly. "I'm sorry, Bronsky. But I can't give you any more jobs."

"But I have to do something, Micky."

"Try with some other agencies."

"They don't know me there. And there's no point. I can't work as a waiter anymore. Or as a window cleaner. And you can't make any money as a dish or car washer."

"I'm sorry, Bronsky."

"I could work as a doorman again!"

"There's nothing available right now."

"Don't you have anything else?"

"Not at the moment, Bronsky."

I was already at the door when Silberstein suddenly called me back. "Wait! I do have something for you, Bronsky."

"What is it?"

"The right job for you."

"The right job?"

"Absolutely."

Micky Silberstein showed me one of the order forms: OLDER LADY LOOKING FOR MAN WHO IS WILLING TO WALK HER DOG.

"So, what do you say to that, Bronsky? It's just right for you. Your legs and hands can tremble all they want. It's not like the dog's going to put in a complaint."

"How much can you earn doing that?"

"The lady pays three dollars for the job."

"I can't live off that."

"You could walk two dogs! I have something else."

"A second dog?"

"Exactly. It belongs to an older gentleman. Also pays three dollars. Two dogs. Six dollars."

"That's not much."

"If you live frugally, you'll get by."

"Okay, Micky."

20.

I worked every day of the week because the dogs had to be walked on Saturdays and Sundays, too. Each of the owners gave me three dollars per day, like Micky had promised. It was easy math: Two dog owners paid a combined six dollars per day. And six times seven is 42. So I earned 42 dollars per week and managed quite alright. And the job wasn't hard. I had to pick up the dogs in the early morning, walk for about an hour so that they got some exercise, and then do the same again in the evening. Of course, I had to make sure that they emptied their bowels and pissed properly.

Wise men say that no job comes without its annoyances. And even this easy job gave me some headaches. The dogs peed on all the cars that were parked at the curb. That often resulted in me getting into trouble with the car owners or chauffeurs, especially on Park Avenue, where the limousines of the rich stood – the Rolls Royces and Cadillacs with their chauffeurs in neat livery, who sat silently at the wheel, waiting. But I couldn't avoid Park Avenue because that's where both dog owners lived. Another problem was the fact that they weren't just dogs but female dogs. One of the dogs was named Candy: a mutt, and not a virgin. She belonged to the older gentleman. Candy's sex didn't cause me any bother, but that wasn't the case with Dolly, the second dog: a white poodle, who belonged to the older lady. It was really bad with Dolly.

"Listen, young man," said the older lady when I picked up Dolly for the first time. "Dolly is a virgin. She's still completely innocent. You have to take care that none of the street dogs jump on her. If Dolly gets pregnant, then you can kiss your job goodbye."

"I'll watch out for Dolly," I said. "Don't worry."

I really did watch out carefully for Dolly. But it still almost happened once. As I was perusing a bookstore's window display, a gentleman with a Great Dane walked by. A male dog, of course. The gentleman stopped next to me. He also seemed to be interested in books. We exchanged a few words about the latest releases. Then – I must have sensed something – I turned around just in time to catch the Great Dane sniffing the butt of my Dolly and, suddenly, mounting her with his stiff cock. I quickly pulled Dolly away from the Dane. Said to myself: Bronsky. That almost cost you your job.

Since taking on the dog walking job, I was able to manage my free time better. I didn't write at night anymore but in the afternoons, ate my meals at the doctor's prescribed times, and went to bed early to be fit for my dog walking job. The attacks became less frequent since I had gotten used to the insulin and started living a routine life. I was more or less content. I lived frugally, avoided the street whores, took cold showers to calm down my cock, which was still functioning, and thought about how THE JACKOFF was making good progress in the hours of day despite the lack of nightly inspiration.

One day, Bronsky, old boy, you will have finished it. One day, the last line of THE JACKOFF will be down on paper.

Sometimes I met Mr. Selig at the emigrants' cafeteria. He always greeted me politely and pretended he didn't know that I had secretly moved out without paying the back rent. I assumed that he didn't tell the landlady about our encounters.

Once he said to me: "You're writing during the afternoons now?"

"Only during the afternoons."

"You seem to be leading a bourgeois life?"

"Depends on how you look at it, Mr. Selig."

"When will you be done with THE JACKOFF?"

"I don't know yet."

My sleazy hotel was crawling with cockroaches. I even found the critters in my bed. A few times I tried to smoke them out with a spray, but they always came back.

I bought the emigrant newspaper and studied the "apartment for rent" ads. Finally, I found what I was looking for.

Another room with an older Jewish lady. Cheap, too.

"My husband died," said the older Jewish lady. "And the kids are married and live far away. You know how it is."

"Yes," I said.

"It's not even about the money. I just don't want to be alone. I'm afraid, you see?"

"What are you afraid of?"

"Of burglars."

"I can understand that."

"So much happens in this city."

"Yes," I said.

"That's the reason why I didn't want a woman. I wanted a man because that makes me feel more secure."

"Understood," I said.

"Are you afraid of burglars?"

"No," I said.

"You can do what you like here," said the older lady. "You just can't receive any lady visitors."

"Okay," I said.

"But you can use the kitchen, the fridge, the bathroom. Even the television."

"You have a television?"

"Indeed, I do. A brand new one."

"Where is it?"

"In the living room."

"And you don't mind if I sit in the living room?"

"On the contrary. That makes me feel less afraid."

I immediately took the room. Said to myself: Man, Bronsky, you really hit the jackpot here. You can even use the television. Truth be told, you've never owned such a thing. Now you don't have to go to the movies anymore. You can save your money. Now you can go to the movies for free. In the living room. At home.

I really was looking forward to enjoying the television.

My diet was expensive because I had to eat mostly protein. That meant meat, fish, and cheese. The medication also cost money. To make ends meet with my 42 dollars, I already had to do without pretty much everything that I occasionally turned to for a bit of fun, most of all street whores, dance bars, and movie theaters. I used to read a lot but recently I hadn't felt like doing that either – I seemed to be lacking the inner calm – and I only glanced through the book reviews in the newspapers to keep up to date. The television was a kind of escape, one that at least offered some distraction.

My landlady went to bed early at nine o'clock. So, night after night, when she was asleep, I sat there alone in the living room, turned the television on, selected the desired program, and stared at the tube.

There was one program that I found particularly enthralling. It ran once a week under the title PSYCHOLOGICAL HOUR. The star of the program was Mary Stone, the most famous psychologist in America.

I never missed it. Every week at 10 o'clock sharp, it was just me and Mary Stone. I remembered everything she said. I knew every wrinkle of her face, every rehearsed gesture, the sound of her voice, the look in her eyes, her friendly, impersonal smile. The only thing I didn't know was how she smelt.

Once a week – between 10 and 11 o'clock – Mary Stone told Americans how to become happy. She talked about the secret of success. According to newspaper reports, her program was the most watched in all America. Millions watched Mary Stone and listened with bated breath.

There was talk of Mary Stone everywhere. Even at the supermarket. Not long ago, when I was in line at the checkout, waiting to buy a carton of discounted cigarettes, I overheard two women behind me whispering: "Did you watch Mary Stone yesterday?"

"Yes."

"Isn't it extraordinary?"

"A genius of a woman!"

"How old do you think she is?"

"About 35."

"Did you get what she said?"

"Of course. There's no more aging, she said. You are as old as you feel."

"Isn't that fabulous?"

"Yes."

"So, I'm not 65. I'm 25."

"Exactly."

At night I dreamt of Mary Stone. I heard her words: "Those who believe in themselves have the world at their feet! – Those who radiate love are beautiful. – Those who are in love do not have to count their wrinkles in the mirror. – Choose the right partner and you won't have problems in your marriage. – Let two days and two nights pass before you make an important decision. – If you are unsociable, don't blame others. – Always think carefully about what you wear. – Try to eat healthily. – Avoid any kind of stress. – Remember that life is short. – If your car annoys you, exchange it and if you don't like your job, then find another one. – Try to laugh heartily at least once a day. – Be sure to have regular bowel movements. – Try to smoke less. – Breathe deeply more often during the day, even with regular air conditioning. – If your stomach is upset, use the Mary Stone method to settle it: Think of something nice. Then you don't need to take any Alka-Seltzer. – Don't accept your fate. Be happy and confident. If things don't go as planned sometimes, think of all the poor people who are not as fortunate as you are to live in this beautiful country. God loves America because America is His field, a sacred field, that rewards the successful with all His love. If you are unsuccessful, don't accuse God's field but yourself.

Ask yourself: What's the matter with me? What happened to my self-belief? Everyone has opportunity here. To find the key to success, you must look within yourself. Don't despair. For, as it is written: 'Seek and ye shall find!' "

I imagine writing a letter to Mary Stone:

Dear Mary Stone,

I, Jakob Bronsky, cannot afford a psychiatrist. Not even a psychologist. I therefore ask you, out of the goodness of your heart, to help me with my problems. Can I come to your practice? When are your office hours?

Sincerely
Jakob Bronsky

The answer came after a week:

Dear Mr. Bronsky,

Who do you think you are? I, Mary Stone, am the most famous psychologist in America. I have millions of fans: Hundreds of thousands write me letters. Everyone wants something. What on earth are you thinking? How can I deal with everyone personally? That's impossible. Everyone has problems. Believe me.

Look here, dear Mr. Bronsky. I have five secretaries that do nothing but toss all these letters into a row of waste baskets. But by strange coincidence, dear Mr. Bronsky, your letter fell to one side: not into but next to one of the many waste baskets – onto the floor. One of my secretaries then accidentally pushed your letter under the rug where it was found the next day by the cleaning lady, who was vacuuming. And the cleaning lady, dear Mr. Bronsky, took your letter – because she didn't know what to do with it – and put it on my desk. And so you see, dear Mr. Bronsky, that's how I ended up reading your letter.

So, look, dear Mr. Bronsky. I'm terribly sorry. First, I'm too busy and, second, it's against my principles to treat anyone who can't pay for free.

Sincerely yours,
Mary Stone

Dear Mary Stone,

Many thanks for your letter. You know, not long ago I met a frigid woman. She came to my apartment and I, Jakob Bronsky, made her happy. With one of my many little tricks. She had a real orgasm. With me, Jakob Bronsky. Well, what do you say about that? Wouldn't you like to give it a try with me? Of course, I have one condition: If I succeed in making you happy with one of my many little tricks, then you, in return, have to treat me for free! Because I, Jakob Bronsky, urgently need a psychiatrist or a psychologist.

Sincerely yours,
Jakob Bronsky

Telegram: Dearest Jakob Bronsky. Read your letter, again through coincidence. Finally! You're the man I've been waiting for my whole life. You know my problem. If you keep to your word, then I'll gladly treat you for free. Leave your television turned on tonight. Right after my show, I will step out of the screen and slip into your bed.

Yours,
Mary Stone

Diary entry: I, the bum Jakob Bronsky, don't know for sure if the poet Jakob Bronsky knows that these letters, and the telegram, too, only exist in his imagination. The only thing I'm sure of is that tonight Jakob Bronsky won't turn off the television.

She came late. When she stepped out of the screen, I heard a clock strike somewhere. Midnight. "In a fairy tale," my mother once said, "midnight is always the witching hour." – Mary Stone darted into my room and slipped into my bed. I fumbled around a bit and soon knew what was wrong with her. I mentally ran through all those little tricks of mine, chose the right one, and treated her.

"So," I said after she had orgasmed. "How do you feel?"

"Like I've been reborn. I've never experienced anything like it."

"You see? You just needed a trip to Jakob Bronsky."

"Jakob Bronsky," Mary Stone whispered.

"I gave you the right treatment!"

"Yes, Jakob Bronsky."

"And now you have to keep your promise!"

"And that would be?"

"Now you have to treat me!"

"As a psychologist?"

"As a psychologist!"

"Do you wish to be analyzed?"

"I do!"

"Tell me anything at all, Jakob Bronsky."

"What am I supposed to say?"

"Anything."

"But I don't know what."

"Start with your childhood."

"That's too boring."

"Then go even further back."

"How far?"

"To a place beyond your memories."

"That far?"

"Or even further."

21.

"In the beginning, there was fear," I said. "Actually, it was warm and cozy in my mother's womb. And still I was afraid. Terribly afraid. It was as if I knew then, as a tiny embryo, what awaited me outside. As if I knew that the moment of birth was also a death sentence. I clung to the umbilical cord of my mother, resolved neither to grow nor to let myself be simply tossed out into this world.

My mother must have sensed something. She held her hands folded over her big belly as if she wanted to pray together with me. 'Dear God,' whispered my mother. 'I want little Jakob to stay like this forever. Have mercy on him. He's gripped by such a strange fear. I can feel it. Make him stop growing. Let him stay inside me forever. I'll keep him warm. I'll be good to him. And I'll nourish him with my blood.' "

"Did Almighty God answer your mother?"

"I don't know," I said. "But I know that my mother answered in His place."

"What did she say?"

" 'It won't work,' " she said. " 'No mother in this world can keep her child forever.' "

"What else did she say?"

" 'She won't even be able to keep the child as long as she's alive, and that's no eternity.' "

"Life is short."

"Exactly."

"Even mothers must die."

"Yes."

"That's why it wouldn't have made sense."

"Exactly. It wouldn't have made sense. I thus had to get out of her womb to live for a while and die one day, either before or after my mother.

When the contractions started, I pushed my little head forward a bit, but it didn't really work because I was lying all twisted. I gave it everything I had. And, finally, I made it. My mother screamed. My head straightened, slipped forward, I opened one eye, the left one, and, for a split second, I caught a glimpse of this world."

"What did you see?"

"At first, I only saw my father, the chain-smoker. He stood next to the bed, smoking, and looked at my mother's belly, fascinated. I also saw the midwife in a white apron. She had huge hands that I was afraid of, because I knew these hands would soon grab me, Jakob Bronsky, to pull me into the shambles."

"What shambles?"

"The shambles that we call 'earth.' "

"Continue."

"I also saw the large, crooked mirror of the bedroom dresser, in which the window was reflected."

"Which window?"

"The window of the bedroom that looked out to the garden."

"Was someone standing at the window?"

"Yes. By the window. Not in the room but outside in the yard."

"So, you lived on the ground floor?"

"Exactly."

"Who was standing there by the window?"

"Two men stood in the yard and looked through the window."

"What kind of men?"

"Two Nazis."

"Were there Nazis at that time?"

"Yes. They were already around."

"What year was that?"

"1926."

"Continue."

"The two Nazis stood there in full uniform, with swastika arm bands and all the bells and whistles. They stared at my mother's belly and talked to each other."

"What did they say?"

"One of them said: 'I bet it will be a boy.' And the other one said: 'I think so, too.' "

"What else did they say?"

" 'It will be a Jew,' said the one. 'I'm sure about that.' 'Why?' said the other.

'Because the parents are Jews.'

'Oh, okay.'

'See.'

'Listen,' said the first one again. 'When he's big enough, we'll stick him in the gas chamber.'

'Which gas chamber?' asked the second one.

'Any,' said the other one."

"Were there already gas chambers in 1926?" asked Mary Stone.

"Not yet," I said.

"And could the two Nazis know that one day there would be gas chambers?"

"Not really," I said.

"So, why did they say it then?"

"I don't know," I said.

"And you claim to have heard and seen all that in a fraction of a second?"

"Yes," I said.

"Continue, Jakob Bronsky," said Mary Stone.

"I pulled my little head back in right away," I said, "because I didn't want my mother to scream. She calmed down immediately, breathed regularly, lay on her back, wiped the sweat off her forehead, and quietly moved her lips. Then the labor started again and my mother began to groan.

I knew I would be lost if I didn't think of something in the next few minutes. Jakob Bronsky, I said to myself. Think of something. Outwit God.

Like I said: My mother began to groan again. She tried to hold on to me in her mind but her womb was impatient; it didn't listen to my mother but to the voice in space and urgently wanted to get rid of me. – If you don't think of something now, Jakob Bronsky, I said to myself, then it's really the end for you."

"Did you think of something?" asked Mary Stone.

"Yes. At the last minute. I tied a Gordian knot in my mother's umbilical cord, laughed to myself, and thought: There, now you can all bite me."

"And what happened then?"

"Then it was time. I slipped all the way forward. 'Let there be light!' said a voice. And it really became light, although my eyes were still closed and completely covered in gunk. The midwife grabbed me with her huge hands, pulled me toward the daylight, saw the Gordian knot in the umbilical cord, laughed cynically, asked my chain-smoking father to give her the stainless steel scissors, took the scissors, cut the Gordian knot, lifted me up, wiped my face, and gave me a pat on the butt.

Paralyzed with fear, I let out the first cry of life.

My father laughed and almost swallowed his cigarette. The midwife also laughed. And even my mother, who had wanted to keep me, suddenly started laughing. The two Nazis at the window grinned. I was bathed and cleaned thoroughly.

I was swathed in a diaper, colored cloth, and a woolen blanket. I assume they wanted to reassure me that the warm packaging was as protective, soft, and cozy as the womb of my mother. But I wasn't fooled. I screamed, kicked with my little arms and legs, twitched my head, and opened my eyes up wide.

Our apartment was well-kept and clean. But there was something wrong with the baby carriage that stood next to the bed of my parents. It was a present from my aunt whose apartment was infested with bedbugs. As soon as I was placed in the baby carriage, the bedbugs pounced upon me and would surely have devoured me had my father not noticed.

'The boy is screaming differently now than before,' said my father to my mother, who sat upright in bed and looked lovingly at the baby carriage. 'Something isn't right here!'

'Maybe because he's not used to it yet,' said my mother. 'He's never lain in a baby carriage before.'

'Especially not a new one,' said my father.

'Are you absolutely sure it is a new one?'

'Most certainly,' said my father. 'The baby carriage is new but it stood around for a while in your sister's apartment, which is totally infested with bedbugs.'

'You don't think there are bedbugs in the new baby carriage, do you?'

'It's possible,' said my father.

My father bent – cigarette in mouth – over the baby carriage. When he saw the bedbugs, he lifted me up as quick as a flash, ashen-faced, lost his cigarette – but didn't even notice – ran around the bedroom with me, didn't know where to put me down, finally decided on the large washbasin that – already emptied and dried – stood on the floor, and laid me in it.

You can imagine," I said, "what a commotion this caused in my parents' bedroom. The midwife came back from the bathroom where she had sat for quite a long time, supposedly due to severe bellyache. The doorbell had also just rang and my father had to go to the front door to see who it was. Our neighbors came in. Shortly afterwards, the family physician, too, who was always late, and relatives showed up, among them my aunt who had given us the baby carriage. My father ran back and forth, accepted congratulations, shook hands, exchanged kisses, yelled at the midwife, said something about bedbugs, talked about another baby carriage that needed to be procured immediately, talked about baby clothes that needed changing, talked about urgency and danger. My mother was no longer laughing but crying, sitting upright in the nuptial bed.

'What is going on here?' asked the midwife. 'Why are you so agitated, Mr. Bronsky?'

'Because the baby carriage is full of bedbugs. And now our Jakob's clothes are, too, as well as the cloth and the woolen blanket.'

'Then we just have to replace them.'

'Yes,' said my father. 'But fast.'

Everyone marveled at the bedbug bites on my skin. The family physician, too. He applied a lotion to my body, then handed me to the midwife, received a schnapps from my father, drank, belched, glanced, with the air of a connoisseur, at the big butt of the midwife, who stood bent over me as she changed my clothes, gave me a new woolen blanket, and carefully wrapped me up. My father ran out of the house, across the street and a little bit further, around the corner, I believe, where there was a department store. He hurriedly bought a new baby carriage, asked the salesman if it was also infested with bedbugs, was reassured when they explained to him that it wasn't, paid, and took the baby carriage with him right away. Soon after, I was lying in my baby carriage again. I had calmed down a bit. I thought: What a fuss they're making just because of a few bedbugs. Thought: Bedbugs aren't important, even though you screamed because it itched so much. Thought: There are more important things in this world – and things that are far worse. Looked over to the window where the two Nazis were still standing and grinning.

My relatives came every day, partly to talk to my mother, but also to admire me. After about a week, my aunt said to my mother: 'Be glad that the bedbugs didn't bite off his little winky.'

'Yes,' said my mother.

'His little winky looks like the little winky of a goy.'

'Because it hasn't been circumcised,' said my mother.

'When will he be circumcised?'

'Tomorrow,' said my mother.

The two Nazis were standing at the window again when I was being circumcised. The one said to the other: 'So that we can recognize him later. He won't be able to convince anyone that he's Aryan with such a mutilated winky.'

'Exactly,' said the other.

'That means he can't escape us.'

'That's right,' said the other.

I was breast-fed by my mother for a long time, even after the circumcision. Later I was bottle-fed.

Being breast-fed was the best time. My mother had large breasts, plump and strong, with round, fleshy nipples. I sucked with delight until I got tired. Then I peed peacefully on the hand that held me, leaned my little head on one of the large breasts, and fell asleep.

Believe me when I tell you," I said, "that Jakob Bronsky was the family's pride and joy. For hours, my parents would sit in front of my bed and stare at me. They couldn't get enough. 'One day,' said my father, 'our Jakob will take over the business.'

'When he's grown up,' said my mother.

'Of course,' said my father. 'When he's grown up.'

'We will pamper him,' said my mother, 'so that he will become your worthy successor.'

'So be it,' said my father.

At the tender age of six weeks, I, Jakob Bronsky, became acquainted with my future role as my father's successor and as future boss of the Bronsky furniture store. My mother dressed me up and was all red in the face as she excitedly pushed me through the streets of our city in the baby carriage. When we arrived in Große Ulrichstraße, the main street in Halle an der Saale, where the Bronsky furniture store was also located, my mother whispered to me: 'Well, Jakob. In a moment you will see your store. Don't soil your diaper. Don't fall asleep again. Show that one day you will be a real boss!' You can imagine how flattered and proud I was. I really tried hard not to fall asleep again or to soil my diaper, kept my eyes open, stayed alert – the future boss – straightened up in my baby carriage, tried to read all the signs above the doors and windows of the stores, then recognized my store, the Bronsky furniture store, leaked a few drops into my diaper, purely out of excitement, but stayed in control and said to myself: 'Jakob. Not now! What are the employees going to think of you if you enter the store with a dirty diaper!'

My mother quickly pushed me across the busy street, through all the people – some with, some without baby carriages – and narrowly past a ringing street car. On the other side of Große Ulrichstraße, she stopped, panting, then summoned her energy and pushed the baby carriage all the way to the store.

My arrival seemed to have made everyone at the Bronsky furniture store giddy with excitement. The employees nervously ran around, the customers twitched, dared only to whisper, and stared at me. Only my father pulled his tie tighter and lifted me out of the baby carriage, radiant with joy.

I was presented to everyone, even to the customers: 'This is Jakob Bronsky, the future boss!'

22.

Our maid had eloped with a railroad employee shortly before my birth. For some time, the maids of our relatives came over to clean our apartment. My aunt took care of the cooking while my mother was confined to bed. Of course, many maids came forward for the job but as my mother was very particular, we sent them all away again. Only when I was seven weeks old did we find the right one. Her name was Grete.

Grete had even larger breasts than my mother. When we were alone, I was allowed to play with them. In return, I let her fiddle with my winky, especially when she bathed me or changed my diaper.

The older I got, the faster time seemed to pass. Soon I started crawling on all fours; shortly after that, I started to practice walking, and one day, I, Jakob Bronsky, stood upright on both legs.

When I was two years old, my mother became pregnant again. In the beginning she tried to fool me into believing that she had gained weight, but then, when I saw her in her maternity dress, I became suspicious. Said to myself: Jakob. The competition is growing in your mother's womb!

And that's how it happened. My mother gave birth to a second son. His name was Abel. Abel was the exact opposite of me. He had black hair, dark eyes, and brownish skin. I hated him from the first moment I saw him.

As soon as Abel was born, I, Jakob Bronsky, future boss of the Bronsky furniture store and successor to my father, was totally neglected by my mother. She seemed to have forgotten that I even existed. She hugged and kissed my brother Abel all day, nursed him, let him sleep between her large breasts. I noticed that Abel behaved exactly like I had when I was as small as him.

One morning I decided to kill Abel. I sneaked up to his baby carriage, noticed that he was asleep, got one of the embroidered sofa pillows from the living room, came back, and pressed the pillow against his mouth and his nose until he was as dead as a doornail."

"I don't believe that," said Mary Stone.

"What don't you believe? That I had a brother?"

"No," said Mary Stone, "That I believe. But I don't believe that his name was Abel and I don't believe that you killed him."

"Believe what you like," I said.

"Keep talking, Jakob Bronsky!"

"What should I tell you?"

"A real story."

"What do you mean?"

"A story that doesn't lie beyond your memories."

"Where should I start?"

"With your first memory!"

"The real one?"

"The real one!"

"My first memory is playing Ring Around the Rosy. I must have been in our yard, in Bernburger Straße I believe, where we lived. I danced with other children whose faces I've forgotten. I only remember that I fell down and started bawling. Then I heard the voice of my mother and the voice of our maid. Someone lifted me up. I think it was my mother."

"Is that all?"

"That's all."

"Well, I find that extremely boring."

"I'm sorry.

I also remember a little girl who lived in the apartment next door. Once I caught her peeing. I was a bit older then.

She was squatting next to the large garden wall. I walked over and stared because I could not understand why she was squatting on the ground to pee. I saw that she didn't have a bird and was astonished.

I asked: 'Where is your bird?'

'What bird?'

'Well, your bird.' I said.

'I don't have a bird!'

I showed her mine. 'You see, I mean this kind of bird.'

The little girl started crying.

Once I went into the forest with Grete, down below, where the Saale River flowed, not far from Giebichensteiner Castle. We weren't alone because Grete had brought along her boyfriend, a streetcar conductor. He was a tall, skinny guy who always grinned. He wore a large visor cap that he sometimes took off and put on my head for fun.

I remember: It was gloomy in the forest. The sun was hidden. Grete spread out a long woolen blanket over the moss. All three of us sat down on the blanket. Grete's boyfriend, the streetcar conductor, took a bottle of schnapps out of his jacket pocket. He grinned, drank – a lot – and then gave Grete the bottle. Later he let me taste the schnapps, too, grinned even more because I started to cough, and took the bottle away from me again.

Then they both got undressed and fucked right in front of me on the woolen blanket. I saw that the streetcar conductor also had a bird, just like me, but his was larger and uncircumcised.

A few days later, I met the little girl again who had peed along the garden wall. I told her what had happened in the forest between our maid and the streetcar conductor. I said: 'Grete has a bird. But she has hidden it in the hole between her legs. That's why the streetcar conductor stuck his bird into Grete's hole – to look for Grete's hidden bird. Because one bird looks for another.'

'Did the streetcar conductor find Grete's bird?'

'Yes.'

We have to do it the same way,' I said to the little girl. 'I'm sure you have a bird, too. It's just hidden. I will find it with my bird and get it out.'

The girl nodded. And then she started bawling again, just like the first time when I had caught her.

'No need to bawl,' I said. 'We'll find your bird.'

The little girl nodded, but then she became afraid and ran away.

I remember my first day of school and the large, blue paper cone packed full of candy that my father had bought for me. My parents accompanied me to school. I clutched the candy bag tightly in my arms. It wasn't far to school. We walked slowly and my father had put his arm around me. I was very proud of my large, blue cone of candy.

Once we had arrived in the classroom, I noticed that some of the children didn't have candy bags. My father explained to me that those were the poor kids whose parents couldn't afford it."

"That's all pretty insignificant," said Mary Stone. "Don't you have anything else to tell me?"

"It's been too long," I said. "My memories have faded."

"Tell me something important!"

"For example?"

"How Hitler rose to power!"

"I can't remember that. I was still too little."

"But you were born in 1926. In 1933 you were seven. One has usually seen a few things by the age of seven."

"Yes, some things," I said. "But it's not much."

"What did you see?"

“As I was walking home with my bag of candy, there was a street fight between Nazis and Communists taking place close to our house. My father was very pale. My mother, too. We went home quickly and locked our front door.”

“That was before the assumption of power?”

“It was shortly before.

When Hitler rose to power, my father said that the Jews would be worse off now. My mother cried and my father tried to console her. He said: ‘This nightmare will be over soon and *he* will surely be overthrown again.’ I also remember our maid, Grete, coming into the living room and reassuring my father that she had ended things with the streetcar conductor *because he had decided to become a member of the Party the day before.*

Initially, at school, it seemed almost as though nothing had changed in Germany. Our teacher gave a speech that none of us understood. He said something about blood and soil, living space, and provision of work, all things that none of us were interested in. One of the boys asked the teacher if there would now also be new soccer balls for the poor kids, but the teacher didn’t know. A swastika flag was now flying above the schoolyard, which I actually thought looked quite neat. Some of my schoolmates’ fathers wore a brown uniform. One of them – the father of the boy who sat next to me in the classroom – laughed every time he saw me … I assume because I was blond and blue-eyed and looked more Aryan than all the other children in the class … he patted my head and gave me a piece of chocolate.

Our teacher didn't say anything about the Jews. Things only changed when he was reassigned and we were given a new teacher. He said that the Jews were to blame for the humiliation of the German people, that the Jews were sitting on their sacks of gold, and that they were bleeding the Germans dry. He told us about the lost war, about the confirmed stab-in-the-back myth, about the international Jewish conspiracy, and about their malicious laughter. The boys in my class didn't understand it either, just as they hadn't understood the other teacher's talk about living space, blood and soil, and provision of work. The only thing we found interesting was the story about the sacks of gold. One of the boys said that he wanted to sit on top of a real sack of gold, too, and another one asked whether it had anything to do with the flying carpet in One Thousand and One Nights, but the teacher didn't know.

Of course, no one in my class knew I was Jewish. But one day word got out. I think because Grete, our maid, who still picked me up after school in the beginning, told the teacher that I had to stay at home the next day because it was a Jewish holiday. The news spread quickly. None of the boys had ever seen a Jew because there weren't many in our town, and because the few who were there weren't recognizable as such. The boys looked at me curiously and turned their heads when I came into the classroom early in the morning. They asked me if I sat on a sack of gold at home, and when I said I didn't, they hit me in the face, disappointed. Of course, I hit back, which made the whole thing even worse.

Now I had to fight with the boys every day. I bit and scratched and kicked. I had wrapped iron wire around my fists to be able to hit back with more power and greater success, but it was no good. They attacked me in packs and beat the living daylights out of me. At home, Grete washed the blood off my face.

My teacher had the most fun with me. Since he had found out I was a Jew, he always thought up new ways to get at me. Once he drew a pig on the blackboard. Then he pointed to me and said: 'Bronsky. Do you know what that is?'

I said: 'A pig.'

'That's a Jew,' said the teacher.

'That's not true,' I said.

'Yes, it's true,' said the teacher. He grinned and added: 'Do you know why the Jews don't eat pork?'

'No,' I said. 'I don't.'

'Because a pig doesn't eat its own.'

'But we do eat pork,' I said, 'because we're not religious.'

'That's not true,' said the teacher.

'Yes, it is,' I said. 'It's true. Only my grandparents don't eat pork because they're pious people.'

'They're pigs,' said the teacher.

'They are not pigs,' I said.

'Look here,' said the teacher. 'Are you contradicting me?'

'Yes,' I said.

'Do you know what happens when one contradicts one's teacher?'

'No,' I said.

'Then I will show you,' said the teacher.

The teacher had a long, thin cane. I had to bend over, but in a way that all the other boys could see my butt. When he beat me, the boys laughed. I didn't want to cry and clenched my teeth. But then I burst into floods of tears.

By then the teacher was beating me almost every day. There was always some pretext. Grete applied a thick balm to my butt.

23.

My mother once told me that my father had fought for Germany in World War I, but in the army of the great Kaiser Franz Joseph, who was allied with Germany. She also showed me the many medals that my father had received for his bravery and patriotism, and told me that my father was a hero.

One morning my father came to my school to take the teacher to task. He wore his officer's uniform and all the medals that my mother had shown me. He asked the teacher how it could be that the son of a brave officer was so mistreated in school. He showed him all his medals but the teacher only laughed and said: 'Similar medals and similar uniforms have been fraudulently acquired by Jews.'

I asked my father if all Jews were rich. My father then told me that there were also many poor Jews, especially in Eastern Europe.

'And in Germany?' I asked.

'Here, too,' said my father, 'but not as many as in the East.'

'Our teacher told us the other day,' I said, 'that all Jews eat garlic.'

'We don't eat garlic,' said my father.

'Why?' I asked.

'Because it gives me heartburn,' said my father.

'And the other Jews?' I asked.

'In the East,' said my father, 'they eat a lot of garlic. But the *goyim* there eat it, too.'

'What are *goyim*?' I asked.

'Those are the non-Jews,' said my father.

This conversation between me and my father took place in the presence of our maid Grete, who happened to be busy with her needlework in the living room. Grete said: 'My former boyfriend, the streetcar conductor, went to Italy once. And there they eat garlic, too.'

'That's true,' said my father. 'The Italians eat a lot of garlic.'

'Even more than the Eastern Jews?'

'I think even more,' said my father.

During gymnastics class, we had to march for a quarter of an hour while singing marching songs. One of the songs that our teacher had taught us was particularly popular among the boys. They always sang it: 'When the Jewish blood spurts off the blade, we've got it made …' I was beaten up because I didn't sing along.

I found it hard to believe that there had been only one national anthem in the past: In school we sang two. And we had to raise our right arm as we did. It was painful and I always got a cramp. So, I said to myself: Bronsky. Two anthems, that takes too long. You will only raise your right arm during one. Otherwise you get cramp. Being as stubborn as I was, I stuck my right hand in my pocket during the Horst Wessel Song. I only raised my right arm during the Song of the Germans. Raised it right. Raised it high.

I remember the large-scale boycott of the Jewish stores. The Nazis had daubed all the windows of the Bronsky furniture store with Stars of David and swear words. Two Brownshirts were stationed in front of the store entrance. They didn't let in a single customer. They had also hung a sign in front of our door: DON'T SHOP IN JEWISH STORES!

My mother cried frequently and my father's face was etched with worry. Once, when Grete picked me up from school, she told me that the Brownshirts had now also smashed the windows of the Bronsky furniture store.

Brownshirt columns now regularly marched along Bernburger Straße. Somehow that had something to do with the time of year and the fact that there were several public holidays. I watched them from our living room window. Once I even saw a torchlight procession during the night.

It was on a Sunday. I had spent the entire evening playing in the children's room with my model electric train. My parents weren't home and Grete was at the neighbors'. I went to bed around nine. I was just about to fall asleep when I heard marching music. I got up, sneaked silently to the window, barefoot. I leaned on it, in my nightshirt, shivering. The torchlight procession marched down the dark street. I was in awe. I had never seen anything like that before. It was as if all the thousands of lit torches were showing the silent, black sky what blood and soil were.

Grete told me that many people were going to concentration camps: Jews, Communists, and others. 'One came back once,' she said. 'He was mere skin and bones, had burn marks from the cigarettes that the guards had put out on his back. He also had only one eye left.'

'Is he the only one who came back?' I asked.

'Another one came back,' said Grete. 'But he couldn't speak anymore.'

'Why?' I asked.

'He came in a little packet,' said Grete, 'that was sent to his wife. He was only a heap of ashes.'

My father's face became more and more lined with worry. Grete told me that we hardly had any customers left because people were afraid of buying from Jews. She also said that she'd have to leave us because Jews were no longer allowed to have servants who were under 45.

'How old are you?' I asked, but Grete didn't want to tell me.

We had to let Grete go. Grete cried and said she would come visit us often.

When we were no longer able to keep the business going, my father sold the Bronsky furniture store in Große Ulrichstraße. He leased a shabby store in the old town that he also called *The Bronsky furniture store*. Shortly afterward, we swapped our nice, large apartment in Bernburger Straße for another one in Königstraße, which was just as little and as shabby as the new store that my father still called *The Bronsky furniture store*.

My teacher said that Jews no longer had a place in Germany. Curiously, my relatives said the same thing, although they phrased it differently. Only my father firmly believed there was hope of a revolution.

Once, after we had moved, I eavesdropped on a conversation in the living room of our new, shabby apartment.

'It's high time to emigrate,' said my uncle. 'The Nazis will beat us all to death.'

'The foreign countries will not allow it,' said my father.

'They won't ask the foreign countries.'

'A revolution will come eventually,' said my father. 'The German people have their eyes open.'

'They don't have any eyes,' said my uncle. 'The German people are totally hypnotized.'

'Listen, Nathan,' said my uncle to my father. 'Word is that the Nazis want to confiscate all of the Jews' assets.'

'I don't believe it,' said my father.

'Word is also,' said my uncle, 'that Jews will soon have to wear a star so they can be recognized on the street, too; that Jews won't be allowed in the cinemas anymore, or in the theaters, won't be allowed to use certain streets, or park benches, or public toilets, or public baths, or even the streetcar.'

'Who told you that?'

'A high-ranking Nazi.'

'How do you know someone like that?'

'He used to be one of my customers.'

'And you believe someone like that?'

'I do.'

'Soon it will be too late to emigrate,' said my uncle. 'Because once the stream of refugees gets too large, most countries will close their borders. You know how that goes. And when our assets get confiscated, no country will want us anyway because most countries already have their hands full with their own proletariat. Without capital you can't immigrate anywhere.'

'Maybe to America,' said my father.

'Then you'll have to hurry up.'

'Why?'

'Because the Americans have a quota system and only issue a certain number of immigration visas per year. If there are too many seeking refuge, there will obviously be more refugees than valid visas. The Americans stubbornly cling to their quota system. You can't negotiate with them either. There's no point. If you don't make it, you get left in the lurch. Then you won't be able to go to America.'

'Perhaps,' said my father.

'What will you do, Nathan?'

'Nothing at all,' said my father. 'I'll wait.'

'There will be a revolution,' said my father. 'Just you wait. Sooner or later the Germans will realize that Hitler wants war. And who wants to go to war?'

'You're wrong about that,' said my uncle.

'You think so?'

'I think so.'

'There will surely be a revolution,' said my father. 'One day you will admit I was right. Everything will be fine again. My customers will come back. I'll sell the shabby store in the old town and lease one in Große Ulrichstraße again. I'll rebuild the old Bronsky furniture store, you see. Just like it was. Everything will be fine again. After all, I have to think of Jakob. Of his future. One day Jakob will have to take over the furniture store.'

'Which Bronsky furniture store?'

'The one in Große Ulrichstraße.'

And then came *Kristallnacht.* The hopes and dreams of my father were dashed for good. The synagogues burned in Germany. My father's store was totally demolished and our apartment was set on fire. The Nazis spit in my father's face and kicked him in the balls. I don't know if my mother was raped. I only know that her dress was torn and full of blood.

The next day my father decided to emigrate.

The day after *Kristallnacht,* my father wrote a desperate letter to the American Consul General and explained our situation. The answer to the express letter didn't come until months later."

"When?" asked Mary Stone.

"In July 1939."

"What did the American Consul General write?"

"That we should be prepared to wait several years before we could expect immigration visas. There was a form attached to the letter that had a preprinted text in addition to the usual questions."

"What did the preprinted text say?"

"More or less the same. My father saved the form and still has it to this day. I know the preprinted text by heart: 'We hereby inform you that the wait time will be several years. Oral and written inquiries to civil servants to expedite your case are futile.' "

"And all that shortly before the gates were closed?"

"Shortly before the gates were closed. When war was imminent."

"When the trap was beginning to close on you?"

"Exactly. When the trap was beginning to close on us inexorably."

"The trap! What did the trap promise … the trap that was not yet totally closed?"

"The extermination of the Jews of Europe. The Final Solution."

"Firing commandos and gas chambers?"

"And much more."

"But it hadn't gotten that far yet?"

"It almost had."

"So, you couldn't emigrate?"

"We could no longer emigrate legally."

"What did you do?"

"We fled across the border."

"Where to?"

"That I will tell you later. It doesn't matter. The war quickly caught up with us."

"What happened?"

"And then came the war," I said. "And the war caught up with the Bronsky family. With Jakob Bronsky, too. And when the war was over, there were suddenly two Jakob Bronskys."

"Why were there two Jakob Bronskys?"

“There were two,” I said. “The one Jakob Bronsky, who died with the six million, and the other Jakob Bronsky, who survived the six million.”

“Tell me something about the two Jakob Bronskys!”

“Which one should I start with?”

“It’s best to go in order.”

“With the first one?”

“Yes. With the first one.”

“The one that died with the six million?”

“The one that died with the six million.”

24.

"The first Jakob Bronsky is only a thought," I said, "a thought that I chased away long ago because I was afraid of it. If the first Jakob Bronsky could still speak to me today, he would tell me the following story:

'I, the first Jakob Bronsky, am only a thought. I lived in six million bodies until their names were erased. Once I flitted into the body of a fourteen-year-old. There I lingered for some time. His voice became my voice, his story … my story.

We lived in Poland, in the part that was, at that time, occupied not by the Germans but by the Russians. My two older sisters had married Russians and had moved far away. One of them to Moscow, the other to Odessa. Only I, the youngest, had remained at home.

My father was a craftsman and worked in a state-run business. I still went to school. My mother was paralyzed and confined to a wheelchair.

On June 22, 1941, my father woke me up very early. I believe dawn had just started to break. He said: 'There's a war, boy. The Germans are coming.'

'That's impossible,' I said. 'We have a nonaggression pact with the Germans.'

'They are coming,' said my father. 'There's a war. I just heard it on the radio.'

I got up and quickly got dressed.

'You have to leave,' said my father. 'Take the bicycle and ride to the train station. Maybe you can still catch a train.'

'Where to?' I asked.

'East,' said my father.

'There's only one way left. Go to your sisters, either to Odessa or to Moscow. The Germans won't advance that far.'

'And you?' I asked.

'We'll stay,' said my father.

'Maybe all three of us can make it to the train station?'

'That wouldn't do any good,' said my father. 'The trains are surely overcrowded. There's no room for a woman in a wheelchair.'

'You're right,' I said. 'Mother is in a wheelchair. It will be hard to take her.'

'Hurry up,' said my father. 'There's no time to lose. And don't worry about us. I'll watch over Mother.'

I took the bicycle and rode toward the train station. I heard bomb blasts coming from the direction of the station. Flames shot up into the sky. When I arrived, the train station had been destroyed.

Since it was now impossible to get a train to anywhere, I rode my bicycle to the next highway. There it was hard to get through because the highway was clogged with many refugees.

I rode my bicycle along a trail. Every once in a while, I encountered units of the Red Army that had set up positions in the surrounding area. Because I was only fourteen, and looked even younger, they let me through.

The Ukrainian border wasn't far from our little town. I made it safely across and arrived in a small town whose train station was still standing. There I caught a train crowded with refugees. I left the bicycle at the train station.

We rode for several hours. Then the train was bombed. I jumped off and continued on foot. Toward evening, I reached a mid-size Ukrainian city.

My father had pressed some money into my hand as we were saying goodbye. It wasn't much. I bought something to eat. At night I slept on a park bench.

The next morning, I met an old man who was peeing near my park bench. I asked him if it was far to Moscow, and he said it was very far.

I went on my way again. Since the city's train station was destroyed, I walked. I chose to head to Moscow because I thought that was safer than Odessa.

I don't know how many days I traveled. One evening I arrived at another mid-size Ukrainian city. There I also slept on a park bench. I woke up in the middle of the night. I heard the sound of grenade blasts. Somewhere on the outskirts of town a battle was being fought. But since I was so exhausted, I fell asleep again. The next morning the city was occupied by the Germans.

There were many Jews living in the city. It was almost like in the small and mid-sized cities of Galicia. I recognized the Jews immediately, and they recognized me. I talked to them and told them my story. The Jews gave me food because I was out of money and because they didn't want me to go hungry; they were friendly to me and understanding. One Jewish family offered me shelter. Because they were poor and only had two beds, I slept on the bench by the stove. But they were good to me, gave me a pillow and a warm blanket, and also shared their bread with me.

The Germans searched every house in the city, but they didn't hurt us. One of them gave me a cigarette. For hours, we stood in front of our houses or at our windows and watched the heavy tanks roll by. But three days later, things changed. That's when the SS came with its *Einsatzkommandos.*

The *Einsatzkommandos* chased the Jews out of the city. I don't know exactly how many Jews, but I estimate there were around five thousand.

There was a forest near the city. A part of the forest had been burned down. That's where they chased us to. We had to dig our own graves and then we were shot.

But I wasn't dead. I wasn't even wounded. That's because when my turn came, it was already almost evening. We had lost a lot of time digging our own graves, and, of course, shooting five thousand people isn't quick work. So, it was already late in the day and the Germans were growing impatient and started to take less care when they aimed. As quick as a flash, I flopped down into the mass grave without the Germans noticing.

There weren't many men among the five thousand because most of the men who were fit for military service had moved off with the Red Army. It was mostly the elderly, women, and children, a few sick people, of course, and a few boys my age. The dead fell on top of me, whole mounds of them.

I lay right underneath a child. It was a little girl of around six or seven. I was drenched in so much of her blood I could hardly breathe.

When darkness fell, the Germans withdrew. I waited until I was sure they were gone. Then I worked my way out of the mound of bodies. The dead formed a kind of staircase, so it was easy to climb out of the mass grave.

For a whole night, I wandered through the forest. Then, at sunrise, I walked aimlessly through the open fields that lay behind the forest.

The Germans were everywhere now, and I was afraid to enter any village. I washed myself in a brook, rested in the shade of a weeping willow, and fell asleep. When I awoke, the sun was already high in the sky.

A farmer told me that Odessa had fallen. When I told him that I wanted to go to my other sister in Moscow, he laughed at me.

I knew there was no point in walking on. I also felt a sudden longing to see my parents and started to worry about my mother. What would she do if something happened to my father? Maybe she needed me? After all, she was paralyzed and confined to a wheelchair.

I walked back to Poland to find my parents. Many weeks passed. I avoided the highways and mostly stayed in the forest. When I came to an area where there was no forest, I walked in a low crouch as I carefully made my way across pastures and fields.

I lived off the fruit in the yards at the edges of the villages. I dug potatoes out of the fields or picked the green, unripe corn cobs. Now and then I killed a bird with a stone or caught little fish in a creek with my bare hands. Sometimes I sneaked into some village at night to steal eggs, bread, and matches from the farmers.

The farm dogs always barked when I broke into the farms. But that didn't bother me because I was quick and long gone by the time the farmer woke up and stumbled sleepily out the door. Only once did I almost get caught. The farmer ran after me, yelling. As I ran across the village square, I saw German soldiers and Ukrainian militia. I jumped over a fence, ran on, and disappeared into the darkness.

I made it across the Polish border unharmed. When I reached the suburbs of my home town, I met an old woman. I asked her if anything had happened to the Jews in the town.

'Nothing special,' said the old woman. 'The Jews are now living in a ghetto.'

'Where is the ghetto?'

'In the eastern part of town.'

I made it into the ghetto by fooling the guards. There were corpses lying on the streets: some in the gutter, some in the middle of the road. Others also lay peacefully in front of the old houses. I asked a Jew if the people had been shot but he said they just starved.

'Don't you have anything left to eat?'

'We don't have anything left to eat.'

'How come?'

'The ghetto has been sealed off. The Germans aren't letting any food in.'

The house that we used to live in was outside of the ghetto. Since my parents weren't living there anymore, I had no other option than to search for them where they were probably staying: in the ghetto. I searched all day, combed the ghetto, building by building, until I finally found my mother. Just her. She was living in a mass shelter. She was sitting in her wheelchair and looked at me when I came in through the door.

'Your suit is covered in blood, my boy. Where on earth have you been?'

'Among the dead.'

'And are you really back?'

'Yes. I am really back.'

'Where is my father?'

'They shot him.'

'That can't be true.'

'Yes. It is. He wanted to get out of the ghetto to find food on the farms. And that's when they caught him.'

I cried softly for a while. My mother stroked my head and comforted me.

'I will look after you now,' I said. 'Don't worry. I'm back now.'

'I only have enough food for four days. Then there will be nothing left.'

'Do you still have some money?'

'I still have some money.'

'Then give it to me. I will go to the villages and buy food.'

'If they catch you outside, they will shoot you.'

'Don't worry. I'll be careful.'

I sneaked out of the ghetto and went to the neighboring village. When the Germans saw me, they asked for my papers. I ran away and they shot at me.

I hid in a field where I was found by Polish farmers. They beat the living daylights out of me and took my money.

What was I supposed to do? I didn't want to go home empty-handed. Somehow I had always managed to get by. But I wasn't alone anymore. I had to take care of my mother now. I couldn't let her starve. I couldn't let her die.

At night, I broke into a Polish farmer's house. I took a few chickens, wrung their necks, and was about to run away. But this time I ran out of luck. The farmer was waiting for me outside the chicken coop, holding a large club.

I desperately tried to defend myself, but the farmer was stronger. He beat me unconscious and left me lying in the courtyard.

When I woke up, I heard the voices of the soldiers from afar and the voice of the farmer who had called them. I looked for the dead chickens, but they had long been hidden by the farmer. I had to act fast. I climbed over the courtyard wall and ran out into the night.

I hung about the area for three days and three nights without being able to secure the food I needed so my mother wouldn't starve. I didn't dare break in again but instead went begging from door to door in the villages. Sometimes the farmers gave me a piece of bread or let me have a spoonful of their soup, but no one gave me any chickens or sacks of flour even though I explained to them that I needed provisions for a week or more so that my mother wouldn't starve. The farmers laughed at me, some chased me away and said I should beat it fast, otherwise they would call the soldiers.

On the fourth day, I got lucky. I told a farmer that I'd give him my shoes and my jacket for a week's supply of flour. The farmer agreed. He gave me the flour and took my shoes and jacket. I went home barefoot and without a jacket.

When I returned to my hometown, the ghetto was no longer there. The Polish Christians told me that the ghetto had been liquidated. I still went to the eastern part of town to see if it was true.

It was. The living Jews were no longer there. Only the dead ones were lying in the streets. The windows of the buildings had been smashed, doors forced open. In the streets, alongside the dead, lay ripped-open mattresses, prayer books, and all kinds of trash. I asked one of the Christians, who was busy looting the apartments, where the living Jews were. He said they took them to the train station.

On the way to the train station, I stopped an old woman. I asked her whether she had seen a transport of Jews. She said: 'Yes.'

'When was that?'

'Yesterday.'

'Did you notice anything?'

'Nothing special. They were just Jews.'

'Did you happen to see a woman in a wheelchair?'

'Yes. As a matter of fact, I did.'

When I arrived at the train station, a conductor told me that although the Jews had been there, the soldiers had moved them on.

'Where to?'

'To another train station.'

'Why?'

'Because the tracks were recently blown up by partisans. All the tracks around the train station.'

'Do you know which train station the convoy of Jews was taken to?'

'Yes, I do,' said the conductor. And he showed me in which direction they went.

I came to a highway. I walked fast because I wanted nothing more than to catch up with my mother. Still, I stopped once to ask a farmer whether he had seen her.

'Did you see a convoy of Jews that came through here yesterday?'

'Yes. I saw it.'

'Did you notice anything?'

'I didn't notice anything.'

'Did you happen to see a woman in a wheelchair?'

'Yes. As a matter of fact, I did.'

I was glad because I was on the right track. I was still carrying the sack of flour on my back. I told myself: Surely my mother found a kindhearted person to push her wheelchair. I couldn't imagine that it would move all by itself.

I walked for a few hours and arrived at the right train station. I asked a conductor: 'Did you see a transport of Jews yesterday?'

'Every day there are transports of Jews,' said the conductor. 'They come from all directions. There was one yesterday, too. This morning as well.'

'Did you happen to see a woman in a wheelchair on any of the transports?'

'Yes. As a matter of fact, I did.'

'What happens to the transports?'

'Not much. The people all get onto the train and go off in a specific direction.'

'In which direction?'

'That way!' He showed me.

'They all go in the same direction?'

'They all go in the same direction.'

I said to myself: If they all go in the same direction, then surely they all go to the same destination. All you have to do is wait for the next transport of Jews. You will get on the train with them and follow your mother. In the same direction. To the same destination. This simple solution is sure to bring you back together.

And that's what happened: When the next transport of Jews arrived, I got on the train with them. The doors were bolted and we departed. We traveled for one day and one night. Then we arrived there, at the destination.

The doors were flung open. Soldiers chased us out of the cars with whips. I wanted to ask one of them if he had seen my mother – a woman in a wheelchair – but I didn't get the chance. They chased us with barking dogs through the large camp gate.

Because I looked younger than I was – I barely even looked fourteen – I was immediately selected for the gas chambers. I had to take off all my clothes and stand in the long line of people in front of the gas chambers.

They pushed us into the gas chamber until we were tightly packed together. As the door to the gas chamber closed, I asked a man standing behind me: 'Did you happen to see my mother? A woman in a wheelchair?'

I repeated my question. But then I couldn't breathe anymore. We started coughing, and I never received an answer.'

25.

I could tell you six million stories," I said to Mary Stone, "but the night isn't long enough. I believe all the nights of a lifetime wouldn't be enough to tell you every single story."

"No one can live to see that many nights."

"That's why I only told you one, just one."

"Let's not talk about it anymore," said Mary Stone. "Let's talk about Jakob Bronsky."

"The second Jakob Bronsky?"

"The second Jakob Bronsky! Who did not die with the six million! Who survived them! And who is now lying next to me!"

"The second Jakob Bronsky," I said, "fled across the German border in 1939 with his mother and his younger brother."

"I thought you didn't have a brother? Because you had killed him? When you were barely three?"

"That was only a story. A nightmare, I guess."

"You said that he was called Abel then?"

"No. His name was Menachim. Then. Later we called him by a different name."

"What name?"

"Achim. Just Achim."

"So, you fled across the German border?"

"Yes."

"With your mother and your brother?"

"With my mother and my brother."

"But without your father?"

"Without my father. He stayed behind in Germany."

"Why?"

"I can't remember why exactly. I think it was because of my grandparents who weren't able to emigrate and later perished in Theresienstadt. At the time, they lived in Leipzig. My father had to take care of them. He was supposed to follow us later, but then the war broke out and he was cut off from us.

I always imagined that we had spent the war in Halle an der Saale. Hidden. In trash cans or in a basement. My brother wasn't with us. Only my father, my mother, and me. But that's not what happened."

"What did happen?"

"Something else.

No country wanted to take us in 1939. That's how it was. The whole world had conspired against us. There was no one who reached out to us. I'm talking about the Bronsky family and others who shared our fate."

"Yes," said Mary Stone.

"All we could get was a visitors' visa to Romania where we had relatives. But the Romanians didn't want us either and soon tried to deport us."

"Yes," said Mary Stone.

"Nevertheless we managed to stay in Romania until 1941."

"How did that happen?"

"The Romanian farmers were open to bribery. At least at the time. We had run out of money and were destitute. But we had rich relatives. You know what I mean?"

"Yes," said Mary Stone.

"My relatives were able to renew our visa. From year to year. Until 1941."

"Yes," said Mary Stone.

"But by 1941, we no longer needed to extend our stay."

"Why?" asked Mary Stone.

"Let me explain," I said. "In Romania, a fascist government had taken over that conspired with the Nazis. In October 1941, all of the Jews were deported from the outer Romanian regions of Bukovina, Bessarabia, and Northern Moldavia, the regions where we and our relatives lived."

"Where were the Jews deported to?"

"To the East."

"Where in the East?"

"To the Ukraine. Into the areas where the mass executions were taking place."

"But you weren't shot dead?" said Mary Stone.

"No," I said. "The large-scale mass executions took place further east. Our transport didn't get that far. Not quite that far anyway."

"How far?"

"We only got to Mohyliv-Podilskyi, a Ukrainian city under Romanian administration. A few kilometers further, almost all the Jews were shot by the SS right after the invasion, but in our sector, it was a bit different."

"Different how?"

"We were locked up in a ghetto. A ghetto is a kind of pre-hell."

"What kind of a pre-hell?"

"A cordoned-off part of the city where the dead lay in the streets, similar to the dead in the other ghetto that I told you about earlier. Only our ghetto was much larger."

"Go on."

"They completely cut us off from the world around us. Starvation and typhus were rife in the ghetto. Almost every night there were raids. If you were caught, you were carried off somewhere and shot."

"Were you afraid?" asked Mary Stone.

"I was afraid."

"Were you hungry?"

"I was hungry."

"Did you freeze during the winter?"

"I froze during the winter."

"Did you have hope?"

"Sometimes," I said. "During the nights of desperation, there were still sometimes moments of hope."

"Did hope keep you alive?"

"Hope kept me alive."

"How long were you there?"

"Almost a thousand days."

"Can you remember each one of those days?"

"I can't."

"You don't want to."

"I don't know."

"You've repressed all that?"

"I have repressed all that.

And yet it's not completely true," I said, "although I always claim to have a huge hole – or, should we say, a gap – in my memory. I'm writing a book, you see. And as I write, lots of things are coming back to me."

"You're writing a book?"

"I'm writing a book."

"About life in the ghetto?"

"About life in the ghetto."

"About the mass dying?"

"About the mass dying."

"About the desperation?"

"About the desperation."

"Are you also writing about hope?"

"I'm also writing about hope."

"Nothing else?"

"Nothing else … except about the loneliness that each one of us carries around. Myself included."

"You're writing down everything that you repressed?"

"I'm writing down everything that I repressed."

"Must you write?"

"I must write."

"Is it very important?"

"It is very important."

"So, you don't want to tell me what you experienced in that ghetto during the war?"

"I only tell that to my book."

"Only to your book?"

"Only to my book."

"Then tell me how it was when the war was over."

"There isn't much to tell."

"You had all survived?"

"Not all of us. Most of my relatives were dead."

"Your mother and your brother?"

"They had survived. Just like me."

"Tell me."

"I told you there isn't much to tell.

When the war was over, I looked in a mirror for the first time in years. My face had no expression, my eyes were empty. I was also mute. Completely mute. I didn't say a word. Not a single word. When people spoke to me, I either nodded or shook my head, depending on whether the question ought to be answered with yes or no. People thought I was a little crazy.

As a boy, I had sometimes written poems. I tried to write again but I couldn't.

Shortly after the war, I met a girl. She was young and beautiful. I think she felt sorry for me. We went to bed together. But nothing happened. Absolutely nothing. My sex drive had vanished. Nothing stirred. I, Jakob Bronsky, was done for.

Then, shortly after the war, I went to Palestine on one of the first refugee transports. My mother thought I'd heal there. In Palestine, I worked in several kibbutzim and also planted trees in the Negev Desert. Later I was drawn to the city. I went to Haifa and found a job as a dishwasher. For a while, I also tried my luck in Tel Aviv and found work in a hospital. Nothing had changed. I did my job but I remained mute."

"You didn't tell me," said Mary Stone, "who liberated the ghetto."

"The Russians liberated it," I said.

"And did the Russians let you travel to Palestine, just like that?"

"Yes," I said.

"And your mother?" asked Mary Stone. "And your brother?"

"They stayed in the Ukraine," I said. "Later they went back to Romania, to the place where we had lived until 1941."

"And then?" asked Mary Stone.

"Then my mother found out through the Red Cross that my father was alive."

"Where was your father?"

"After he had been separated from us, he fled to France. There he went into hiding during the war."

"Your mother found his address?"

"Yes, that's right."

"Your father then came to her?"

"No. It was the other way around. After the war, my mother traveled to him. With my brother, of course."

"They traveled to France?"

"Yes."

"Legally?"

"No. In the meantime, the Iron Curtain had been raised. They crossed the border at night. First to Hungary. Then to Austria. At some point, they arrived in France. There was a veritable mass migration going on in Europe. It was nothing special."

"In what city did you find your father?"

"In Lyon."

"The city on the Rhône?"

"Yes, exactly."

"And you, Jakob Bronsky. You were in the Holy Land and remained mute?"

"That's how it was."

"Didn't you want to see your father again?"

"Of course."

"Your father came to Palestine?"

"No," I said. "When my mother wrote telling me where my father was, I also traveled to France."

"So, the Bronsky family was reunited?"

"That's right. The Bronsky family was reunited.

At first, my father was happy to see me," I said.

"But when he noticed how sick I was, he became bitter.

One day my father dragged me to a sanatorium. There they admitted me right away. They treated me with electric shocks and medication. When I was released, I was in an even worse state than before."

"What did your father do in France?" asked Mary Stone.

"He was still dreaming about the Bronsky furniture store that he would rebuild one day. But truth be told, he didn't have the energy for that anymore. He worked in Lyon as a small-time salesman for a clothing company and supported our family as best he could."

"And what did you do, Jakob Bronsky?"

"I lived off my father's money. I had no desire to work nor to do anything else that was useful."

"But you must have done something?"

"I went to the public library and read all kinds of books."

"And what else?"

"I went on a lot of walks."

"Did you ever see any girls?"

"Once in a while," I said. "I even went to bed with a few of them. But truth be told, nothing real ever happened."

"Nothing real? Don't be shy, Jakob Bronsky. Spit it out!"

"You know what I mean!"

"Your cock stayed limp?"

"Yes, exactly. My cock stayed limp. Nothing stirred."

"Jakob Bronsky was done for?"

"Jakob Bronsky was done for.

One day we moved to Paris," I said.

"Did anything change there?"

"Nothing changed there.

I then lived in Paris but hardly noticed the city. Do you understand? I lived there with my memories and my fear.

In 1952, we all went to America. Suddenly it was easy to get immigration visas. We were considered 'displaced persons' and the Americans didn't cause us any difficulties. But it was too late, you see. It was too late."

"Because Jakob Bronsky was done for?"

"Not just because of that. Somehow we were all done for. We weren't the same anymore. Deep down, my father was also a broken man, although he didn't want to admit it."

"The Americans should have saved you in 1939?"

"That's right, Mary Stone. They should have saved us in 1939.

I had neither gone to school nor learned anything about how to make a living. So, in New York, I also took every job I could get. One day I began to write.

And suddenly I became healthy again. I don't know if you can understand this, Mary Stone. But when I had finished the first chapter of my ghetto book, I was healthy again. Everything that had been dammed up suddenly flowed freely out of me. The more I wrote, the freer I felt. I started speaking again, came across as a rational human being, could suddenly make jokes, suddenly had a sense of humor again. And something else."

"What else?"

"My sex drive reawakened. I suddenly said to myself: Bronsky. It's working again."

"Your cock had awoken?"

"Exactly."

"From its long sleep?"

"Yes."

"It got hard again?"

"Yes."

"I can understand that, Jakob Bronsky. I can understand that very well."

"I slept with women again, although they were only street whores, but I had no difficulties."

"Jakob Bronsky was no longer done for?"

"Jakob Bronsky was no longer done for."

"Do you know, Jakob Bronsky, what a pupil of Freud once said?"

"No, Mary Stone."

" 'A man's soul is healthy when he can get his cock up.' "

"And how is it with women?"

"Similar, although women, as you know, don't have cocks."

"That's right, Mary Stone."

"That's right, Jakob Bronsky."

"You are right," I said to Mary Stone. "I am healthy again. But I still have problems."

"Everyone has problems."

"But mine are especially difficult."

"You only think that. Everyone believes that his problems are the most difficult."

"Mary Stone," I said. "I have understood that it is not enough to merely survive. Survival is not enough. I have learned that the birth of every living being is also a death sentence, and I'm wondering what the point of it all is. Why am I alive?"

"To search, Jakob Bronsky. To search."

"For a hidden meaning in all this meaninglessness?"

"Yes, Jakob Bronsky."

"Maybe the point of life is just for us to search?"

"I don't know, Jakob Bronsky. But maybe one day you will find out."

"I can't see your face, Mary Stone. Because it is too dark. But I think you're laughing at me!"

"I'm not laughing at you, Jakob Bronsky. I'm only wondering if you're suffering from *Weltschmerz.*"

"I'm grown up, Mary Stone. Why would I be suffering from *Weltschmerz?* Maybe it's just my fear, a different fear from the one I had back then in the ghetto?"

"Maybe, Jakob Bronsky."

"Mary Stone," I said. "I have other problems, too, problems that are more practical and have nothing to do with my primal fear."

"What kinds of problems are those?"

"The practical problems of an unknown and destitute writer, but most of all, of a German writer of Jewish origin in a foreign country – in a country that I don't understand and that doesn't understand me."

"America is a land of promise!"

"America is a nightmare."

"Maybe for people like Jakob Bronsky?"

"That's right, Mary Stone.

26.

I imagine returning to Germany, despite not having forgotten anything. Not a single thing.

I arrive at the train station – the train station of a large German city. Filled with astonishment, I notice that even the luggage porter speaks my language.

I don't feel at home. No one knows me in this city. Still, I don't want to go to Halle an der Saale because no one knows me there anymore either.

I stroll through the streets. My language is being spoken everywhere. It somehow feels good. I try not to think about the six million.

There is a small Jewish community in this city. I go to the community center and speak to a friendly man.

'So, you are Jakob Bronsky?'

'I am Jakob Bronsky.'

'Do you have family in Germany?'

'I have no one here.'

'No family at all?'

'Yes. They're in America.'

'Where?'

'In California.'

'Your parents?'

'Yes.'

'Siblings, too?'

'One brother.'

'Where?'

'Also in California. He is married and has a good job.'

'That's wonderful.'

'I think so, too.'

'Does your family want to return to Germany?'

'No.'

'But you have returned?'

'Exactly.'

'Do you have an occupation?'

'No.'

'Got any job skills?'

'No.'

'Do you want a job?'

'No.'

'But you have to do something?'

'I'm writing a book.'

'A book?'

'A book.'

'What's the title of your book?'

'THE JACKOFF.'

'You can't be serious?'
'Yes, I am.'

'We can't do anything for you here, Mr. Bronsky. But I'll give you an address. These people are very helpful.'
'Would they also help a poor writer?'
'Yes.'
'What kind of people are they?'
'They're the Guilt and Atonement Association.'
'Guilt and Atonement?'
'Guilt and Atonement.'

The secretary general of the Guilt and Atonement Association, who looked like an old Nazi out of uniform, cried when he saw me.
'We are delighted, Mr. Bronsky, that you have returned to us.'
'I am flattered.'
'Didn't you like America?'
'No.'
'Would you like to stay here?'
'Yes.'
'Have you forgotten the six million?'
'No.'

'Why would you like to stay here?'
'First and foremost, because of the language.'
'Any other reasons?'
'Because I don't like it in America.'
'You already said that.'

'Yes.'

'Other reasons?'

'To see if the Germans will change.'

'Is that an allusion to our new democracy?'

'It's no allusion at all.'

'Can you wait?'

'Yes.'

'We need time.'

'I know that.'

'Time is important. I'm thinking of the next generation.'

'Of those yet to grow up?'

'That's right, Mr. Bronsky.'

'I'm especially interested in this next generation.'

'Do you really have time to wait for them?'

'I have plenty of time.'

'Would you like a job, Mr. Bronsky?'

'They asked me that at the Jewish center, too.'

'Would you like one?'

'No.'

'Please don't take this the wrong way, but perhaps you would like to do something to earn your daily bread?'

'No. I have absolutely no desire to do that.'

'But you will be bored. You have to keep busy somehow!'

'I will work on my book.'

'You are writing a book?'

'Yes.'

'We will do everything for you, Mr. Bronsky, to ensure you have an easy and comfortable life. As far as we are concerned, you need neither a job nor to do anything else.'

'Glad to hear it.'

'That's what our association – the Guilt and Atonement Association – is there for.'

'Thank you very much.'

'We will rent an apartment for you and, of course, pay your rent,' said the secretary general of the Guilt and Atonement Association. 'You will receive an atonement care package from us daily with all kinds of delicious treats. Your physical well-being will thus be taken care of. In addition, you will receive spending money, and if you need anything else, please let us know.'

'I need a new suit and a coat, as well as shoes, underwear, shirts, and socks.'

'That's no problem. We will send you everything you need.'

'I also like to read,' I said. 'I could go to the library, but I'd rather own the books myself.'

'That also won't be a problem. Give us a list and we will send you the books you request.'

'I also need women,' I said. 'Because that was a huge problem in America.'

'We have plenty of women,' said the secretary general of the Guilt and Atonement Association. 'They are mainly the wives of former SS members, but there are also others who are not guilty themselves but who believe in collective guilt and would like to atone for us all.'

'That really is wonderful news,' I said.

‘That’s what we’re here for,’ said the secretary general of the Guilt and Atonement Association.

I lived comfortably in Germany. My rent was paid and I was sent the finest treats to eat. I also received clothes and book parcels, an allowance, and women. I didn’t want for anything. Since I had plenty of free time, I was able to calmly work on my book until the last line was down on paper and THE JACKOFF was finished.

My manuscript lay in a drawer for years. My hair has turned gray. I am slowly growing old.

One day I wrote a letter to my mother. I wrote: Dear Mother. I am very sorry that I, your son Jakob, disappointed my father so and did not become his worthy successor as he had wished. I’m living rather well in Germany. But I’m sick of this life. Today I will end it. I have destroyed everything I own, with the exception of a manuscript that is locked in the drawer of my desk. On top of the desk, for all to see, lies my will. Yours, Jakob.”

“Your mother came to Germany, no doubt?” said Mary Stone.

“She was already very old. But she came.”

“She found your will?”

“Exactly.”

“What was written in the will?”

“It was written that Max Brod, the man who discovered Kafka, was the only man authorized to open my desk drawer.”

“What did your old mother do?”

"She sent my will to Max Brod."

"Was he still alive?"

"Yes.

Max Brod came to Germany and opened the drawer of my desk. He found my manuscript and read it. Then he spoke with my mother on the telephone.

'Mrs. Bronsky. I read the manuscript. Your son was a genius. A second Kafka.' "

"So then the manuscript was published, of course?" asked Mary Stone.

"Of course.

I once had a relationship with a cleaner who worked in a publishing house in Hamburg," I said. "But because I had *the* Max Brod acting on my behalf, I no longer needed the help of this cleaning lady."

"Tell me," said Mary Stone. "I assume that the man who discovered Kafka managed to sell your manuscript?"

"Of course," I said. "Nothing could go wrong with such an impressive recommendation. The publishing houses fought over my manuscript."

"Who printed the manuscript?"

"I can't tell you. A large German publisher."

"Did the book become a success?"

"A huge success. Jakob Bronsky became famous."

"But he was dead?"

"He wasn't dead at all. Jakob Bronsky took the liberty of playing a little trick with the will and a bad joke on his mother by writing her a letter to torture her because she had once nursed his brother, tenderly, lovingly, with devotion, back then … while little Jakob stood by and watched, totally neglected and alone."

"Go on, Jakob Bronsky!"

"After I became famous, I told the press that I was alive. I reappeared. Do you know what I mean?"

"Yes," said Mary Stone.

"I picture myself – me, Jakob Bronsky, the famous writer – arriving at the train station of another German city, a city that is even larger than the city where I live. All the media bigwigs are gathered on the platform. As I step out, a red carpet is rolled out at my feet.

A taxi takes me to the largest television studio. The media people follow.

I'm sitting in the television studio. Millions of Germans can see and hear me.

Interviewer: 'Mr. Bronsky! Right now, millions can hear and see you!'

Bronsky: 'I know.'

Interviewer: 'Why did you write your book?'

Bronsky: 'To heal.'

Interviewer: 'Didn't you also want to become famous?'

Bronsky: 'Actually, yes. That, too. Although I wasn't conscious of it in the beginning. But, you know, I've always had certain complexes and so I could do with a good dose of fame, and, of course, all the dough that's coming my way, too.'

Interviewer: 'The critics are saying you write even better than Kafka. Say, where did you study German literature?'

Bronsky: 'I read a ton of books.'

Interviewer: 'That's not studying German literature.'

Bronsky: 'I was also at university.'

Interviewer: 'Which one?'

Bronsky: 'At the men's restroom in Donald's pub on Times Square.'

Interviewer: 'Is that a university?'

Bronsky: 'Yes.'

Interviewer: 'Can you explain?'

Bronsky: 'A huge Negro was standing there urinating. We talked in American slang. That's when I developed the right distance to the German language.'

Interviewer: 'You mean … you became painfully aware of the beauty of the German language?'

Bronsky: 'Exactly.'

Interviewer: 'How did you become a writer?'

Bronsky: 'I've been put through the mill.'

Interviewer: 'By whom?'

Bronsky: 'By life.'

Interviewer: 'Are you talking about the school of life?'

Bronsky: 'Yes.'

Interviewer: 'Mr. Bronsky. Do you have anything to say to the German people?'

Bronsky: 'I have nothing to say to the old people. They already know.'

Interviewer: 'And to the young people?'

Bronsky: 'To the young, I would like to say that they should read my book.'

Interviewer: 'Your book about the Jewish ghetto?'

Bronsky: 'My book that stands against violence and inhumanity.'

Interviewer: 'THE JACKOFF?'

Bronsky: 'THE JACKOFF!' "

www.ingramcontent.com/pod-product-compliance
Lightning Source LLC
Chambersburg PA
CBHW020937310726
48980CB00007B/805/J

* 9 7 8 3 9 4 3 3 3 4 1 1 1 *